Cum for Me 6

Lock Down Publications & Ca$h Whispers
Cum for Me 6

Lock Down Publications
Po Box 944
Stockbridge, Ga 30281

Visit our website at
www.lockdownpublications.com

First Edition November 2020
Printed in the United States of America
This is a work of fiction. Names, characters, places, and incidents either are products of the author's imagination or are used fictitiously. Any similarity to actual events or locales or persons, living or dead, is entirely coincidental.
Cover design and layout by: Dynasty's Cover Me
Book interior design by: Shawn Walker
Edited by: Leondra Williams

Stay Connected with Us!

Text **LOCKDOWN** to 22828 to stay up-to-date with new
releases, sneak peaks, contests and more…
Thank you!

Submission Guideline.

Submit the first three chapters of your completed manuscript to ldpsubmissions@gmail.com, subject line: Your book's title. The manuscript must be in a .doc file and sent as an attachment. Document should be in Times New Roman, double spaced and in size 12 font. Also, provide your synopsis and full contact information. If sending multiple submissions, they must each be in a separate email.

Have a story but no way to send it electronically? You can still submit to LDP/Ca$h Presents. Send in the first three chapters, written or typed, of your completed manuscript to:

LDP: Submissions Dept
Po Box 944
Stockbridge, Ga 30281

DO NOT send original manuscript. Must be a duplicate.

Provide your synopsis and a cover letter containing your full contact information.

Thanks for considering LDP and Ca$h Presents.

Zion

Chapter One

Today felt like it was going to be a great one for me. Whenever I felt like this, something good usually happened. I was on my way to a photoshoot. I was an urban model, and this would be my sixth time being featured in a men's magazine. Ever since I had hired an agent, my career had been going in the right direction. A little more about me, I'm twenty-two years young. Not only did I model, but my main job was dancing, or what most people like to call it, stripping. I danced at the famous Blue Flame in Atlanta. I'd been dancing there for a little over a year now. One of the dancers I was cool with encouraged me to model for swimsuits and lingerie magazines. I'd only been doing it for like seven months. It was good exposure in modeling. My DM used to be alright before modeling. After modeling, oh lord, I couldn't even tell you what it looks like now. I hadn't had the time to read all the messages left by some of my 50,000 plus followers. I didn't have to tell you all the propositions and dick pics that were sent to me on a daily basis. There had been women sending nude photos of themselves. At the club, I met plenty of entertainers ranging from actors, reality stars, singers, rappers, and professional athletes. Imagine all the money that was thrown inside the club. Not to mention, the private dances and, "I'll give you this, if you do this for me," invitations that come attached with it.

It was a headache sometimes because the guy or the girl would request some weird ass sex act, but the amount of money I received, relieved all pain and suffering. You gotta know that! Yes, I've had sex for money. Judge me. Judge me not. If I didn't do it, someone else would. Let's get one thing straight now. I didn't do it because I was forced to, or I was strung out on drugs. I did it because I wanted to. I'm a hustler slash go-getter. Whatever I want, I go and get it, point blank period. I answered to no one. Nobody told me what to do or how to do it. I played by my own rules. If they didn't like it, they knew what they could do. Everything I got, I got it on my own. Speaking of which, I had my own crib. I didn't have a car note because that motherfucker's paid in full and not once had I been behind on my rent. I don't want to sound like I have an exaggerated self-opinion about myself. That was never the case. For the most part, I was a nice person, very humble, with a sparkling personality. I loved to laugh and have a good time. I got along with just about anyone. It was the haters and negative energy I couldn't stand to be around. If I was your friend, then I was your friend. I'd give you my last if it's meant to help you in any way. But don't ever, and I do mean *ever* cross me. You don't know what vindictive means until you fuck me over.

Any who, I pulled up to the location of my photoshoot. I hopped out of my car, looking and feeling like not one, but two million bucks. I entered the building and strutted to the desk where this pretty black girl was sitting behind a computer. I told her who I was, and she told me to wait. No more than five minutes passed before a gorgeous woman with a banging body walked out. She approached me and introduced herself.

"I'm Alisa. We spoke on the phone last week. I'm the talent scout and will also be conducting your interview after your photoshoot. Follow me."

She led me to the set with one of the sexiest walks I had ever seen. Her round, bubble butt looked scrumptious poking out the back of her dress. We got to the set and I looked around, highly impressed with what I saw. It was made up as an all-white bedroom with the king-sized bed. It was dope how professional they were. This was a powerhouse company.

They were the alpha publication company. A moment later, the photographer walked in with his camera.

Oh, my goodness! This man was fine with a capital F! I had to blink my eyes three times to make sure I was not daydreaming. He was tall, caramel skin, with light brown eyes, and a low-cut fade. He had on a button-up shirt, that was only half buttoned. It looked to be Versace. I could see his impeccable chest. *Damn!* I swore my pussy just kicked! Sexy didn't even begin to describe him right. I needed a better word to characterize him. He was in a league of his own. I wished I could take his picture and publish them in my own women's magazine. He would be the star in a lot of lonely, horny housewives' fantasies.

"Hey. Nice to meet you," he smiled and extended his hand.

"Likewise," was all I could muster up.

"I'm Cali, your photographer."

I didn't want to let his hand go, but I had to.

"Would you like to see your wardrobe, or have you brought your own?" Alisa asked, looking at the Louie V bag draped over my shoulder.

I let her know that I had my own wardrobe, but I would use their own makeup artist. Alisa walked me over to the makeup station. I took another look at Cali and shook my head at all that fineness. Just beautiful I tell you. Alisa left me with the makeup girl to go and prep her questions she had to ask for the magazine. Before I got my makeup applied, I went to the dressing room to change into my all pink bra and thong. I put on my robe and flip-flops and returned to the makeup station to meet Ashley, the makeup artist. While she was hooking me up, she let me in on some pretty interesting things that were going on around there. What I learned from her, could unmistakably boost my modeling career. I thought it over for a second. Damn right I was going to use what I knew to get what I wanted, just like I always did. As soon as Ashley was done with me, I started my shoot.

For the first picture, Cali wanted me on the bed, positioned on my knees, while holding out my boobs for the camera. Or was it for him? I held one boob and put a finger in my mouth, giving him my best "Fuck me" eyes. He snapped about three pictures of me in that pose, then suggested that I get on all fours and look back at the camera.

"Place a hand on your butt. That's it. Now, imagine you're having sex with your boyfriend. I need that face you make."

The sound of Cali's voice was driving my pussy crazy. I closed my eyes and opened my mouth the way I did when I was having an orgasm. I screwed my face up and all. As I was doing this, I thought about the size of Cali's dick. I wondered how big it was and how it would feel making love to me or just fucking me silly like a straight up slut. I was so turned on. My pussy was incredibly wet. Could Cali see it? Did he know how bad I wanted him? This man was doing a number on me and he hadn't even touched me. This never happened at any of my other shoots. Cali had me do a few more poses then ended it.

"You were amazing," he said, handing me my robe.

"Thank you." I replied, looking from his eyes down to the obvious bulge in his pants. I knew I had an effect on him. Especially the snaps he took of me on my back with my legs gaped wide open. I knew he could see the outline of my pussy. I could see the lust in his eyes.

"Would you like to freshen up before your interview?" Alisa came from out of nowhere, interrupting the undeniable chemistry between Cali and I. Honestly, I was so wrapped up in Cali's swag that I'd forgotten she was there. She told me they had showers if I wanted to take one. I could definitely use one. I needed to put out the fire between my legs. I told her yes and followed her while we talked about my shoot. There was a stall with four shower heads. Alisa handed me a bag filled with hygiene products. These people were serious about their business. I'd brought my own, so I was straight.

"As soon as you're done here, we can start your interview. I want to give you the heads up on some of the questions I'll be asking. Some will pertain to your sex life."

"Whatever's clever. I'm professional, so I know what to expect. I don't mind answering them. I want people to know how freaky I am anyway," I laughed.

Alisa smiled. "Say no more. I'll leave you to your shower. Have my secretary to show you my office when you're done." Alisa gave me a flirty look before walking out, locking and closing the door behind her.

I turned on the water, setting it to the perfect temperature. I hurried out of my clothes, pressed for time because I was still horny from my photoshoot. I wanted to bust a quick nut so I could feel relaxed. I got under the water and thought about Cali joining me. I fantasized about him bending me over and fucking me good and hard. He didn't talk. He just dominated me. He pulled my hair roughly, pulling me up so he could bite my neck. Oh God, yes! These images were making me rub my clit harder and faster. That was it. I was almost there. I stifled my moans not wanting to be heard by anyone walking by. I went back into my fantasy. I wanted to cum for Cali. I pictured him shoving me over with force, grabbing my hips, as he pushed his cock in and out of me. Meanwhile, five more rubs across my clit, and I exploded. I took two fingers from my left hand and shoved them inside of me. At the same time, I was still massaging my clit. As my orgasm died down, I took the two fingers formerly inside of me and placed them in my mouth.

"Mmmm. So good!" I moaned quietly, wishing it were Cali's cum I was relishing. I sucked my cum from my fingers then finished my shower.

Now that I was relaxed, it was back to business. I dressed comfortably and followed the instructions Alisa had given me. I found her and Cali engaged in a conversation. I wondered if they had sex before. Probably so. Alisa smiled that pretty smile of hers and dismissed Cali from her office. Ah man, I wanted him to stay to hear what I had to say in my interview. I figured I would try to catch him on my way out. Hopefully, we'd exchange numbers. Alisa wanted me to sit on the couch instead of at her desk. We took a seat and she asked if I was ready.

"Let's get it," I said, as she pressed record on her iPhone.

"How are you today, Nikki Bunz? Glad you could make it."

"Thanks for havin' me. I'm great. Super excited about being featured in Urban Heartshapes. Shout out to Yasmin for creating the game's top swimsuit and lingerie magazine."

"She's my sister, so I'll be sure to tell her what you said. Can you tell the readers where you're from?"

"I'm originally from Jackson, Mississippi, A.K.A, Jack-Town. But now I reside here in Atlanta."

"What's your nationality?"

"Most people mistake me for Dominican, but I'm just a white girl with a tan." I laughed. So did Alisa.

"And one with a nice phat ass might I add. I assume that's why you put Bunz at the end of your name?"

"Yep."

"Is it real or have you had work done?"

"Nope. My ass is 1,000% real. I don't know how I got it because no other women in my family have one."

"Guess you can say you're blessed. Your booty definitely looks good on you. You remind me of Kylie Jenner. Only you're redheaded. What's your height and measurements?"

"Last time I checked, I'm 5'5. 36-28-45."

"That's certainly fine. Okay, let's talk sex. What kinda man turns you on?"

"A man with confidence, swagger, and money in his pockets. Last but not least, he has to have some bomb ass head and dick."

"What about size?"

"I enjoy a big dick, but not too big. Sex is meant to feel good and sometimes, a big dick can be rather painful, especially if he doesn't know how to use all that meat. Don't get me wrong, I like a little pain. I like the kind that feels good. So, let's see. Ten inches is great for me."

"I see. What's your favorite sexual position?"

"Depends on the man. Whichever one he feels most powerful in is the one I want to be in. I love being dominated and treated like a slut. Get gangsta with me. Pull my hair. Slap my ass until it turns as red as an apple. Bite my neck. Call me a bitch and a whore. That type of shit will have my pussy leakin' wet."

"Do you give head?"

"Of course, I do. I love it. I'm a dick sucking queen. I don't let no man fuck unless he lets me suck him off first."

"Are you into anal?"

"He gotta eat the booty first if he wants to get back there. I like to ride the dick while it's in my ass, although occasionally, I have let a few men push my legs all the way back to my head and let him get it in like that."

"What about women? Have you ever been intimate with one before?"

"Hell yes! I'm a dancer, so I've played around with a few of them. Women are beautiful and super sexy. I like biting and sucking on nipples. I love the taste of some good clean pussy. I especially love the taste of a women's cum. Yummy!" I watched Alisa twitch in her seat. We held a long, fixed stare with each other as I continued. "Women are the best pussy eaters. I love doing a split over her face, sitting my pussy right on her mouth, letting her eat me like she's at a picnic." Alisa licked her lips then asked me had I ever had a threesome before. I moved my head up and down. "It feels good getting pounded hard from the back while I got a phat pussy in my face. Or getting my clit sucked at the same time I'm being penetrated."

"Have you ever been double-penetrated?"

"Nah. But now that you mention it, I'll put it on my things to do list."

Alisa blushed. I could tell she was turned on by the way she was acting. She kept moving in her seat and squeezing her legs together like she was trying to control her pussy.

"This is by far one of the best interviews I've conducted. What can we look forward to coming from Nikki Bunz in the near future?"

"I have a few business opportunities lined up. What I would like most is to be on the cover of Urban Heartshapes. I would do anything to make that happen." I gave Alisa a suggestive look, letting her know that I was down for whatever to get on their cover. What she didn't know was that Ashley had informed me about the initial cover model being involved in a car accident and she'd suffered a broken leg. Ashley told me Alisa was in search of her replacement. She also told me that Alisa went both ways. That was the most valuable information I could have gotten, because I was about to seal the cover girl spot on this one. I waited for Alisa to say something. She has the prettiest set of lips.

"Thank you for the interview, Nikki Bunz. It was a pleasure talking with. Would you like to leave a final shout out?"

I gave a shout out to all the people who would see my layout. I left my Instagram handle and told them to follow me, then wrapped up my interview. Alisa saved our interview to a file on her phone before walking to the front of her desk to retrieve an envelope with my payment in it.

"Here's your money." We'd agreed to cash payment when we talked on the phone. I walked over to collect and when she passed me the envelope, she touched my hand and began massaging it softly.

"Were you serious when you said you'd do anything to get on the cover, or was it all for show?" She grabbed my hand, pulling me in close. She pushed a string of my hair out of my face then ran her fingertip lightly down the side of my face.

"I'm a businesswoman at the beginning and end of each day. I don't bullshit around when it comes to business," I said in a firm, matter-of-fact tone. We gazed into each other's eyes. "I was dead ass serious when I said it. What do I have to do in order to secure that spot because I want it?"

"I don't normally do this, but you have me so turned on, I can't help myself. I want you to be that nasty little slut you say you are and have a threesome with me and my man." Her breath smelled like tropical Starburst.

"How do I know you'll keep your word if I do it?"

"Just like you, Nikki, I'm a businesswoman twenty-four, seven." She grabbed my butt, pulling me in for a kiss. I kissed her back. I have to say, she was an excellent kisser. Never had I been kissed and the person kissing me made me moan. Maybe while I was being penetrated by cock, fingers, or dildo did it happen, but I can't recall it ever happening like this. Alisa was kissing me like I was her lover. This was just a business transaction. She was getting what she wants, I was getting what I wanted, and we would walk away proud of what we did, and life goes on. I wasn't about to complain though. It was time I put my skills on full display.

I cupped her butt cheeks, backing her up to the desk. I ran my hands under her skirt, feeling her smooth brown skin. I squeezed her soft, juicy butt, kneading it as I gave her my tongue to suck on. Eventually, I fell to my knees, pulling her panties down with me. I spread her legs like a cop, looking up to see her beautifully shaved treasure anticipating my next move. Kissing my way up her leg, I buried my nose in her slit. God, she smelled fabulous. I licked her slowly from her hole to her bud. I swear she tasted like candy. I swiped my tongue again, then stood up and seated her on the desk. I wanted her alone before getting with her man. This would be an added bonus for her. She opened her legs for me. I asked her did she want me to lock the door.

"I already have."

What the hell? I turned around and there was Cali sitting on the sofa with his shirt off and his pants unbuttoned. *When had he come in,* I wondered?

"And I've sent everyone on an hour lunch break," He said, sitting there all handsome, cocky, and delectable. What he was doing here was the real question. I turned my head back to Alisa who was pulling her dress over her head. "He's my man," she explained coolly.

So, the plot thickened. Ashley failed to mention this information. Not that I was trippin'. I wanted to fuck Cali anyway. If only they knew what I'd done in the shower. "Go ahead. Finish what you started," he commanded me.

I happily obeyed him, turning back to find Alisa holding her pussy lips open for me. I took off my Nike spandex suit and thong before bending over and covering her wet mound with my mouth. I tooted my ass high, shaking it for Cali as I feasted away on Alisa's small pearl. I sucked softly, the way she cried out for me to do. Closing my eyes, I zoned out like I always do when I got a delicious tenderloin kitty on my dinner plate. I was doing my thang when I felt Cali's hands on my head. He grabbed a handful of my hair, turning my head to him.

"Oh my!" I exclaimed at the sight of him. He was completely naked, standing there long, thick, and oh so strong. Make no mistake about it, I was up for the challenge. Still holding a fistful of my hair, he forced me down to my knees.

"My turn," he said. I opened my mouth, eager to suck his big, black dick like I'd fantasized about doing in the shower.

"It's so big," I glared at it, worshipping it as I wrapped my hand around the shaft. I couldn't help but kiss all over it. "And so fuckin' hard," I murmured, squeezing my hand tighter. I began slapping his strong cock on my face, gliding his big mushroom head back and forth across my lips, teasing him. He didn't have to speak. His eyes said it all. I opened wide, inserting him into my magical mouth. I rose from my knees, bending over to take him. It was time I put to shame every woman who'd ever sucked his dick, including Alisa. The real MVP was here. I worked his dick greedily, hungry for more. It wasn't long before I swallowed him whole, letting his dickhead rest at the back of my throat.

"Ssshhhhiiiiitttttt!" He cried to the ceiling. I pulled back then quickly swallowed him again, this time shaking my head from left to right. "Gottttdammmmnnnn!" A second later, I felt a stinging slap on my ass. Another second, another one. I screamed around Cali's cock as his hand landed a third time.

I massaged my tongue on the underside of his shaft and moaned at the pleasure of it. The only reason I tore my mouth away, was because I had to breathe. He grabbed my hair again, pulling it to place me back in front of Alisa's glistening cunt. Back and forth I went between them licking, sucking, and deepthroating. I made Alisa cum twice. I would've made Cali bust his load, but he kept running from me. Scared ass. That was alright. He couldn't run much longer. Sooner or later, he was going to give me that nut.

In the meantime, Alisa got off the desk and led me to the couch. I couldn't resist smacking on that perfect round ass of hers. She sat me down and pushed my legs open after going down to her knees. "Pussy so pink and pretty," She muttered and began eating me out exquisitely.

"That's it. Eat my pussy, bitch!" Calling her a bitch seemed to turn her on even more. She moaned around my clit, composing a vibration on it. I pulled the hood of my clit back to allow her better access to it. I looked at Cali who was standing behind her, strapping himself up with a Magnum. "You ready to get in this tight, white pussy? Bring it on! And you better fuck me good!" I said, twerkin' my pussy on Alisa's mouth. I could see the fire in Cali's eyes as he approached. I knew I was about to be the business. He smacked Alisa's ass, signaling for her to move aside. She tongue kissed my pussy a few more seconds before joining me on the sofa to suck on my titties. Cali was on his knees, leveled with my wet entrance. He placed my legs on his shoulders. In one hard stroke, he entered me. It didn't take long for him to start beating my pussy up.

"Cali! Oh my God, Cali! Yes! Yes! Oh, baby, Cali! Yesss!" He had me screaming his name like the bitch I was. Faster, his hips moved in a rhythmic pace. Hard. Harder. Faster. Gotdamn it, I was almost there. Fuck! He had the nerve to pull out. Why'd he do that? "Nooo. Don't stop! Give it back!" I whined.

"Turn that ass around."

I'd never moved so fast for a man in my entire life. Still on the couch, I got on my knees, letting my shoulders touch the seat of the sofa. Alisa pulled open my butt cheeks, smacking them, as Cali entered me roughly to continue his dominance on me. He had me moanin', groanin', mumblin', grumblin', whinin', and cryin' out in unbelievable pleasure.

"Ooouuu. Fu-fuck me! Ooouu, you goin' hard on my pussy, yasss! Get it, baby!"

"You love that black dick, don't you, white girl?" Alisa asked.

"Yes! Oh, my goodness, yesss! Thank you, Alisa!"

"Why are you thanking me?"

"For lettin' your man fuck me with his good ass black dick!"

"Tell him how good he's making you feel."

"Oh, Cali, you're makin' me wanna love you, you big dick mothafucka!" I started throwing the pussy back at him. He took that as a sign to speed up his thrusts, working a pleasure spot in me I never knew existed. He grabbed two fistfuls of my hair, pulling my head back hard, as he speared into me over and over again with his long ass dick. It hurt so good. I knew I wasn't about to last much longer. Not a second passed before I started cumming. Cali was indeed a professional dick slinger, fucking me like I had never been fucked before. I wanted to put him in my Louie bag, take him home with me, and keep him handcuffed to my bed, so I could fuck him on demand. From the way he was breathing, I knew he was about to blow.

"Cum in my mouth, baby. I wanna taste it!"

I did not want him to waste that good nut in a condom. He pulled out of me, taking the latex off in the process. I fell to my knees, panting hard with my mouth open, ready to taste his seed. "Cum for me, Zaddy! Bust it right here. Ahhhh!" I stuck my tongue out while he jacked off in front of me. I began licking his dickhead, fondling his balls at the same time. "Don't you wanna cum for me? All in my mouth? On my pretty face? Give it to me! Mmmm."

The expression on his face was priceless. Spurt after spurt of his warm cum landed on my tongue, some on my lips. I swallowed what was on my tongue then licked off what was on my lips and swallowed that too. I sucked the tip of his dick, making sure that I got every last drop. I heard Alisa whimpering in the background. I turned around. She was fingering herself to another orgasm. I crawled to her, sticking my tongue inside of her as I lapped up her cum, sealing the deal for the cover of Urban Heartshapes.

We only had a few minutes to shower and clean ourselves up before the others returned from lunch. Inside the shower, Alisa and I sucked Cali to another orgasm. I let her swallow his cum this time.

Back inside her office, I told Alisa I looked forward to working with her again. "No problem. I want to put you on some future covers as well. We're thinking about doing an issue with nothing but snow bunnies. You'll be perfect for that cover as well."

"If you promise to replay that scenario, then count me in on all of it. I'm down with it." We laughed.

"Sure thing," she said. "Next time I'm bringing my strap-on, so we can really have some fun. You up for being double penetrated?" she asked me.

"I'd like that." I blushed, kissing her. I'd do anything to fuck Cali again. Before I left, I asked her what date the magazine would be published on. She gave me a date three weeks from the next day and invited me to host the party that every cover model hosted when a new Urban Heartshapes issue came out.

"I got your number. I'll call to remind. Do you have any experience in hosting parties?" I told her no, but that it shouldn't be too hard to learn. She said she would call me in three days so that I could get some practice in.

"Cool. I'll be lookin' for you." I told her if I didn't answer when she called to leave a voicemail, text, or email and I would return her call. We kissed again and I went home.

Days went by. Then weeks. No sign of Alisa. Not one single word. I finally decided to call her. This bitch had changed her number. I went on her Instagram and Facebook pages to message her. She never replied to any of my messages. *Oh, hell to the no!* I know she wasn't taking it there. But as they say, actions speak louder than words.

I kindly made my way back to her office. She was nowhere in sight. Their receptionist or whoever the girl was asked if I wanted to leave a message. I chose to take a seat and wait Alisa out. I'd had it up to here sending messages and shit. I thought Cali would come out, but apparently, he wasn't there either. I spotted Ashley. I cornered her in hopes of getting the information I needed to find Alisa. Ashley wanted to play hardball. I tried to offer her some money for the info, but she refused. She had something else in mind. This bitch made me eat her pussy for it, talking about how she heard us in Alisa's office the day I'd sold my soul to the devil. I followed her to a hotel and tongue fucked the hoe.

The night of the magazine issue release party, I pulled up at Club Onyx, ready to confront Alisa for playing me to the left the way she had. I felt like she didn't have to lie. She and

Cali could have pulled up on me and shot their shots and knowin' me, I would've been game for it. Hell, they could have even paid me to have a threesome with them. I found Alisa and Cali talking to one of the models and confronted them. They were surprised to see me.

"Thank you for callin' me the way you promised you would. I'm impressed at the way you guys handle business," I said with disdain. I turned my attention to the model and dropped some salt on Alisa and Cali. "If they're tryin' to get you to sleep with them, let me warn you now. I had a threesome with them and now I have a STD."

Model girl's eyes bucked as she peered at Alisa and Cali. She shook her head, thanked me for putting her up on game, and walked away leaving me there with these two lying motherfuckers. Technically, Cali didn't lie to me. However, Alisa was his bitch so he may as well have lied to me, too. Alisa pulled me away from Cali.

"That was totally unnecessary. But I'm sorry, Nikki. My sister wanted to go with another girl for the cover."

"Save it, Alisa. You could've talked to me like a woman, but you chose to avoid me like a little girl. Then you had the nerve to change your number. That alone lets me know you're on some bullshit. I told you I'm about my business. If that's what Yasmin wanted, I could have taken an L and dusted myself off and waited my turn. You didn't give me that option, did you?"

"I'm sorry. Let me make it up to you."

"Too late," I said and stormed away.

When I got close to the exit, a few men stopped me so that I could sign my autograph on my layout in their magazines. I couldn't deny my fans even though I wanted to rip every page of me out of that stupid magazine. I left to handle my business. I was a woman on a mission. I went straight to Urban

Heartshapes headquarters and set that bitch ablaze. *Let's see them play their little game with someone else. Ha!* Alongside many spectators, I watched that motherfucker burn to the ground. Nobody fucked over me! No fuckin' body!

Two weeks later, the police showed up at my door and arrested me for arson. *Damn cameras every fuckin' where! Fuck it! It is what it is!* I told myself.

Zion

Chapter Two
Two Years Later...

My arms were wrapped around his neck. My legs rested on top of his shoulders as his balls slapped repeatedly against my backside. A split-second later, he told me to hold on tight. Without breaking his momentum, he stood up with me as he continued laying that big, black pipe into my tight, pink pussy. I practiced the Kegel move I'd learned from the sex book I'd ordered from Amazon last week. I tightened my vaginal muscles around his shaft like the author suggested I do, and I got the results she said I'd get.

    "Mmgh! Grrrr!" Cali groaned into my ear as he stroked me hard and forgiving. "Oooo-ooouuu. Daddy, fuckkkk! Right there feels so good! Keep hittin' that same spot!" I whimpered, kissing his neck.

    "Why you always actin' crazy? Got me fired from my job and shit!" he asked, hammering away at my pussy with vigor.

    "Baby, I'm sorry! Oh God, I'm sorry!"

    "Fuck you!"

    "Yessss! Yes baby, fucccckkkkk meeeee! Oouuu-weee, fuck me!" I wanted him to turn up on me the way he always did when he was disappointed or mad at me. What we were having was pure makeup sex. Whenever I started shit for the hell of it, he always punished me with nothing but pleasure.

    My latest shenanigans had cost him his job working as a cameraman for a popular reality TV show here in Atlanta. I'd heard he was messing around with one of the producers and I barged on the set one day, disrespecting everybody and their mamas. I even beat the brakes off the bitch because she had the audacity to step to me and reveal that she and Cali were indeed fucking around. I was not the toughest female when it came to fighting, but I'd be damned if I backed down from a fight. Especially when it came to mine.

"You say you're sorry?" Cali entreated, hips moving faster.

"Yesss, baby! I'm so sorry! Please forgive me! Please! Mmmmhh. Oh, fuck! Shit!"

In one swift motion, he threw me on the bed, rough and ready. Cali had that beast in his eyes. That long, thick gangsta dick of his throbbed for me. "Face down, ass up!" he instructed, climbing into bed. "

Oh, God," I cried out, assuming the position. In an instant, I felt his lips and tongue on my pearl. Then, his talented tongue worked its way inside my pussy. He stabbed me with it a few times before moving up about an inch to spit in my bootyhole. His tongue flirted with the rim, the tip of it taking a dip inside ever so often. So freaky. So fuckin' nasty. Good gracious, yes! He was preparing to fuck my ass. I loved this man with every breath of me, so it was only right that I gave him all of me. I felt him applying more spit to lube me up. Soon after, I felt his dickhead breach my backdoor.

"Go slow, daddy," I moaned. Evidently, he had his own plans. He didn't go fast, but he entered me strong until I felt his midsection on my ass. I gasped.

My eyes bucked wide at the sound of the guard waking me up to give me my breakfast tray. Out of twenty-four months in this place, I'd dreamt about Cali at least twenty times. Some of those nights would replay the threesome I had with him and Alisa's bitch asses. My dreams were mostly about Cali. I didn't know why because I had no desire to be with him in any form or fashion. I hadn't even heard from him. The only time I would think of him was when I'd reflect on how I ended up doing two years in the first damn place. One thing I found out about myself is that I was only tough outside of a courtroom.

When I was standing in front of that judge knowing he had the power to sentence me to the maximum time for arson, I was scared shitless. I didn't know what was on that man's mind that morning. Had he been in an argument with his wife and was about to take his anger out on every woman he saw that day? What about his kids? Did he leave the house upset with any of them and was about to take it out on my young ass? Or did he just leave the house saying today '*I'm sending everyone who comes in front of me to prison for a very long time*'? I couldn't read him. He had a lukewarm vibe going on. I honestly thought he was going to sentence me to a long time until he asked me if I had something to say. I used that opportunity to cry like my entire family had just died. I cried like a baby, pleading with him that I was sorry for what I'd done and begged him to give me another chance. I didn't go into full detail about what led to my actions, but I did explain how I'd been scammed by some very lowdown and conniving people. I swore to Jesus Christ I would never do it again. My lawyer, who I'd met at the club I danced in, and who I'd also slept with for money on many occasions tried every trick in the book to get me probation. Yes, my payment to him for representing me was sex. So fuckin' what!

Anyway, he reminded the judge that it was my first time ever getting into trouble. I guess the judge didn't take my squeaky-clean record into consideration because he still sentenced my ass to three years in jail, two years of probation, and a $15,000 restitution. This time when I cried, my tears were the real deal.

Three years?! I was nowhere near ready for that. I looked at my lawyer's ol' garbage ass and wanted to slap the shit out of him, literally. While I was suckin' his diminutive white dick, he promised to get me off this shit. Well, at least I didn't have to spend any money on him. I was smart enough to put all my money in the bank a week before court. My friend, Tia, who was also a dancer from the club, put me up on game about the judicial system. She told me just because I was white didn't mean anything because I was a stripper who spent all my time with black people.

"Once that old white judge finds out that you love black dick, what do you think he's goin' to think of you? He's goin' to outcast you, Nikki. I pray that you don't have to do any time at all, but it would be smart on your behalf if you start lookin' both ways before crossin' the street."

"What the hell is that supposed to mean, Tia?" I asked.

"It means you need to put whatever money you got saved up in the bank and let it draw interest, 'cause there's a possibility that you can go to prison. Yasmin's a celebrity and she's out for your blood. Think about it, she knows people."

I took Tia's advice and put my money in the bank. It would be waiting on me when I got out. The bailiff allowed me to hug my family before leading me out. Alisa and Yasmin were there with their supporters. They were all mean muggin' the hell out of me. I didn't see Cali. Yasmin said she was going to pay me back for burning down her business. "Blame your sister, bitch!" I said, not taking too kindly to her threat.

So here I am, getting off my cot to receive one of my hots. I wouldn't say the food is hot. It's so-so. It was two boiled eggs, sugarless oatmeal, a biscuit, and milk. I wasn't big on eating the oatmeal. I only ate the eggs and drank the milk just to put something on my stomach. Good thing I only had a week left in this bitch. I'd checked myself into protective custody a week ago. I wanted to be here so I could use some time alone to think. I didn't want to go back into the world with a scattered brain. I had a plan and I wanted to make sure those were my thoughts exiting prison.

The years I had served were some testing times dealing with these bitches. I couldn't even count how many fights I had been in. It seemed that some bitch always had a problem and wanted to take it out on somebody. I was tested day in and day out, fightin' for my respect. Don't get me wrong, I met some cool ass bitches I would fuck with in the world. But being in this cell by myself, I was able to conversate with God a little. I'd been running from Him on the strength of my lifestyle. I wanted to talk to Him but avoid Him all at the same time. My plans for when I got out weren't considered Christlike. Just being real, I hadn't included church in any of my plans. I was still young, and I wanted to live life to the fullest. I'd worry about settling down maybe in my mid-thirties or early forties, perhaps. Prison and these bitches had made me smarter and had given me more insight about life. I was more balanced now. At least, that's how I felt. They could either hate me or love me. Either way, the world was about to be re-introduced to Nikki Bunz.

Zion

Chapter Three

I wanted to kiss the ground so bad, that's how happy I was to be out. It had been a long time coming. Too damn long to be honest. I did the crime and now I'd done the time. Now all that was left for me to do was complete two years of probation and pay that dumb ass fine, which I thought was ridiculous to begin with. I was going to do everything in my power not to get into any more trouble and pay every dollar I owed to the great state of Georgia, so that I'd be a free woman. I already had my blueprint drawn up on how I was going to accumulate the money. I wasn't too worried about that. That part was covered. Here I was just saying that I wanted to kiss the ground because of how happy I was. When I saw my bestie, my pretty, brown-skinned down bitch, Tia here to pick me up, I was even happier. Tia had rode it out with me every step of the way like a true friend. She accepted my phone calls. She put money on my commissary. She wrote letters and sent photos of us highlighting the fun we used to have. She even came to see me once a month. Tia was a diamond in the rough. She was the most loyal and dependable person I knew. I loved her like a sister.

I'd known her since I moved to Atlanta to live with my cousin, Rachel. She lived next door and we quickly became cordial. Tia used to always make lewd comments about my butt like hers wasn't just as big. She was five years older than me. She was born and raised in Atlanta. She had twin boys, but because of her lifestyle, they lived with her mother. One night we were hanging out at her apartment just the two of us, I asked her what her occupation was, and that's when she told me she was a stripper. I couldn't deny that she had the face of an angel and the body of a goddess. I couldn't find one flaw on her. From head to toe, Tia was a bad bitch. She thought I would be the perfect stripper if there were ever one.

"A white girl with an ass like yours would have niggas throwin' nothin' but them big faced hunnids," she said.

"As much as I like the idea of doin' that, there's one problem."

"What's that?"

"I can't dance." It felt like she laughed at me for a full ten seconds then told me I didn't need to know how to dance. All I needed to know how to do was twerk. "I can't do that either. I mean, I can a little bit, but nothin' like them bitches I see on YouTube," I said, almost ashamed to admit it. Shaking my head, there were men who could twerk better than me.

"Let me see what you got." Tia smiled.

"You mean right here, right now?" Oh Lord, what had I gotten myself into. I knew she would call me out on it. Damn her.

"C'mon, shake it fast, show me what you're workin' with," She egged me on, pushing me to do something I wasn't comfortable with doing.

Tia turned on some music by Future. *Here goes nothing*, I thought and began twerkin' the way I did when I was in front of my mirror just goofing around. Tia busted out laughing so hard, she fell to the floor, holding her stomach. I couldn't help but laugh myself. I knew my no rhythm having ass wasn't on beat. Not even close. I was looking dumb as hell trying my best to twerk all this stiff, white booty. Tia finally got off the floor and took me to school. I was in complete awe watching her do her thang. She was a professional twerker. Not once did she get off beat. She fell to the floor on her knees making her ass move in waves. Shortly after, she hopped to her feet in the squatting position to continue bouncing that ass up and down like a basketball.

I must say, she turned me on. By the time she was done, my pussy was flustered and upset that Tia wasn't gay or bi. Three nights before, she'd made it very clear that she had no sexual interest in women. I don't know why she brought that up when I hadn't made a pass at her, nor had I attempted to flirt with her. After her twerk session, I excused myself to her bathroom just so I could get a couple of whoosah's in. I needed it badly. I returned moments later, and Tia taught me how to twerk. It wasn't just for that one night. No, she would practice with me every day, even taking me to this place where they had stripper poles so I could practice on them too. She really wanted me to become a stripper. Whenever she wasn't around, I was getting all the practice I could. The more I practiced, the more I perfected the craft. When Tia felt that I was ready, she got me a job at the Blue Flame. The rest was history.

Tia was a huge influence on me and my life. She was my big sister. I was with her almost every day, tucked tightly under her wing. She taught me the ins and outs of the club. She told me who to fuck with, who not to fuck with. She showed me who paid the most and who paid the least. It was her idea to add Bunz to the end of my name and then she taught me how to make my name a brand. She said I didn't need to be just a stripper. The dancers got younger by the day. I would only get older, so that meant I needed to think years ahead and not one day at a time.

"Let this club be a key to open up some doors for you even if you gotta open up your legs or give a little head. Fuck who's hatin' on you or tryin' to judge you. They are not the ones who's payin' your bills. If you decide to sell your ass for some cash, there are a few rules. One, make sure you're safe and second rule, get your money before a nigga busts his nut."

"What's the third rule?" I asked her, just knowing there was more to learn.

"Never forget what I just told you." Little did she know, I was definitely in the business of selling pussy. By the time Tia was done being my teacher, I was a straight A student. I was game tight.

I wasn't the only white girl dancing at the Blue Flame, but I was the baddest one there. Tia was exactly right when she said guys would make it rain on me with big face hunnids. It was more like a tsunami with the way money was thrown at me when I performed. I soon became one of the highest paid dancers there. Of course, the hating was turned up to the max, but I paid it no mind at all. I kept doing me and didn't worry myself with other people's problems. There was too much money coming at me to give my energy to that. It didn't take long for the sexual propositions to come knockin'. I only had sex with celebrities and athletes because those were the ones with something to lose if I ended up having to scream rape because they felt they had the power to take advantage of me. The most money I ever received from having sex was $20,000. It was with the star player of the Atlanta Hawks, whose name I won't mention, and two of his teammates. They ran a train on me for six hours straight one night they'd come to the club. They took turns fuckin' my mouth, pussy, and ass. It was crazy. Star player only wanted head. One guy wanted nothing but my pussy, and the other one brought pleasure to my ass.

The next morning, my whole body was sore. It was all worth it in the end. That night with them boosted the hell out of my confidence. If you wanted to have sex with me, it would come at a price. I didn't charge everyone that high. Star player offered that amount and I accepted it. The only one who got it for free was this other black dancer named Shamarah. She was cocoa colored with freckles in her face. We were about the same height, size, and age. She didn't have any kids. That was my bitch, and we had an *I don't know what to call it* kinda relationship like MoneyBagg Yo was talking about in his song. We never got jealous if one of us had sex with someone else, either male or female. We just connected in a bizarre way, and that was fantastic with me. Shamarah was the one who encouraged me to model for swimsuits and lingerie magazines. She felt like I could be successful if I took it seriously. She sounded just like Tia when Tia thought it would be a great idea if I became a stripper.

"You know how many niggas locked up gon' love jackin' off to yo fine ass," Shamarah laughed. "You a white girl with a big booty. Niggas love that. Trust me, you're gonna be great," Yea, I was great alright. So great that it landed me in prison. Anyway, I was happy to be free.

On the ride back to Tia's, Tia was telling me about her new two-bedroom condo on Northside Drive. She said I was welcomed to stay until I got on my feet. I was only planning to stay no longer than a month. That was sufficient time for me to move into my own place. She then told me about her boyfriend, the famous one she always talked about in her letters. He was the one who'd gotten her the condo. When we arrived at her place, she showed me my room. On the bed were a couple of outfits and undergarments she'd bought me. She'd even purchased me a phone. She said that I didn't have to worry about paying her back.

"I know you wanna shower, so you can wash that nasty ass prison smell off of you."

"You have no idea," I replied.

"I feel you. Just remember, this ain't prison so you can't sit up under the water all damn day. A bitch got water bills out here," Tia and I laughed. She was so crazy. Always with the jokes.

"Okay," I said.

After my shower, I dressed. Nothing fancy. Just some skinny jeans, a halter top, and some heels. After I dressed, I got on I.G. and went live to announce to all my followers and fans that Queen Nikki Bunz was back. Tia had to make me log off after so long. She was ready to leave, there was somewhere she wanted to take me. She drove us to the convention center right across the street from the Georgia Dome. We got out and she led us inside where I was taken by surprise.

"Surprise! Welcome home, Nikki!"

My parents, two brothers, and younger sister, Rachel and a few other family members from Mississippi, Shamarah and a few dancers I was halfway cool with were there with plenty of food and beverages. There were some people there I didn't even know at all. It didn't matter, though. I was in high spirits. For the first time in a long time, I showed emotions. My tears trickled down my face in abundance. They say never say never but fuck that. I was saying it loud and clear. I was never going back to prison! This is where I needed to be with the people I loved and loved me. Dorothy was absolutely right. There's no place like home.

Chapter Four

Good thing my parents kept my car for me while I was away. Otherwise, I'd be riding with Marta buses to handle all my business. Let me stop lying. A bitch was way too good for that. Tia or Shamarah would've loaned me their car if I needed it. Today I had to go see my probation officer, then go to the courthouse to set up a payment plan for the $15,000 fine I owed. I was completely surprised at the appearance of my P.O. She was a pretty black woman, average in height, and looked younger than me. She looked like she was fresh out of high school. However, I could sense that she was serious about her job. She told me to refer to her as Ms. Taylor. Her very next words were everything she expected from me. Monthly check-ins, drug tests, payments to her, I had to get a job, etc. She even made me take a piss test before I left. I didn't do drugs, so I wasn't worried about that. She said she wouldn't hesitate to send me back to prison if I violated the terms of my probation. I left there, heading straight to the courthouse. They were making me pay a hundred dollars a month on my fine. Easy peasy.

Before leaving, I sat in the parking lot in my car, going live on Instagram. I was updating my fans on what I'd been doing all morning and afternoon until it got too hot. Even with the A.C. blowing, the sun was blazing like a mothafucka. I needed to get offline anyway. I had business to tend to.

I stopped by the bank to check on my money and withdrew a couple of thousands before I headed over to the Blue Flame to see if I could get my old job back. I mean, why not? I was still young, pretty, thick, and fine. I had kept up my shape while in prison. I wasn't an exercise guru or maniac, I just did enough to keep a tone fit. I made sure I did the right number of sit-ups to keep my stomach flat and plenty of squats to keep me bootylicious. I walked inside the club and was greeted with love by the bouncers, waitresses, and a few girls that were working the afternoon/evening shift. There were some faithful patrons on the scene getting their daily dose of lap dances. As I was making my way to the owner's office, I spotted one frequenter who used to be one of my top supporters. I instantly thought about the last time we were in his suite.

******

The feel of his lips drawing on my tender bud sent fierce, flaming pleasure racing to my pussy. Fire raced through me, jerking my hips, driving my womb against his mouth. I nearly squirted from the intensity of it. I looked down at him, not believing he ate pussy this good. I thought that was only reserved for a woman, but dude right here was putting that myth in a state of uncertainty. The flash of lust was in his beautiful, brown eyes.

"You like the way I'm eating your pretty pussy?" he whispered against my clit. I couldn't answer him. All I could do was breathe. Moan. Pant. Whimper. I felt his fingers sliding into me. My mouth opened wider. Where the hell was his dick? I needed it to fill my mouth so bad. I wanted to moan against his skin. My body shuddered as I stared past my double D's to gaze into his brown eyes. His fingers dug deeper inside of me, tongue and lips pulling and sucking at my bud.

"Fuck! Fuck! Fuck, Devin! That feels sooo gooo-gooood, nigga!"

I don't mean to offend anyone, but Devin liked for me to use the n-word when we had sex. As long as he paid me, I would've called him anything he wanted me to. My fingers clenched his hair. My back arched and rushes of flames tore through my body in a forcible response to this man making me cum. *I fed him my nectar and he ate it up gluttonously like he'd never taste anything as sweet as me. As the final beat of my orgasm flexed on his tongue, he stood up, removing his clothes. All six foot two inches of him was delightful to my eyes. That nine-inch monster of his seemed to have a heartbeat of its own the way it pulsated.*

"Get yo' ass up, bitch!" He ordered roughly, turning me on. "You know what I want." I didn't move. I wanted to tease him first.

"I have no idea what you want. Why don't you tell me?"

"That hot fuckin' mouth of yours. I wanna fuck it."

"You do?"

"Bitch, get yo' ass over here and suck my dick, now!"

"Yes, daddy!" I got on my hands and knees and crawled to the edge of the bed where he stood holding his dick at the base. I swirled my tongue around the engorged head three times, purposely ignoring the pre-cum that was oozing out of him. I licked down the side of his dick, all the way to where his hand rested. I removed his hand in place of mine, taking control of his beast. I let it rest on my face, feeling it throb before I began licking my way to his balls and fondling them with my lips. I was sucking and pulling on them the same way he'd done my clit. I licked my way back up to his dickhead, holding out my tongue, as he slapped his pre-cum on it. So good. I jerked more from it, wishing he would bust already. I wanted more. Fuck all this teasing. I made his dick disappear in my mouth, felt it stretching my throat as I deepthroated nine inches of him. I relaxed my throat to receive the last inch.

"Ssss! Shiiiit! Suck my dick, bitch!" He grabbed my head and fucked my mouth slowly until I pulled my head away.

"Fuck it hard, nigga!" I urged him.

He put a foot on the bed, pulled my head over him, and fucked my mouth like it was a pussy. I gagged and choked, but

I didn't care. I wanted him to go even harder because I was his slutty little porn star. His Kelsi Monroe. His Abella Danger. His Alexis Texas. His cum thirsty, deepthroating bitch who loved getting her mouth filled with black cock and cum. He withdrew from my mouth after thirty seconds of drilling it and grabbed a condom from the bowl filled with them on the nightstand beside the bed. I lay on my back, patting my pussy while he prepared to fuck me in the missionary position. He liked to suck my toes while he long dicked me. Before I met with him, I would always make sure my toenails were painted in his favorite color, red. He had a thing for my feet. Sometimes he would make me give him a foot job so he could bust his load all over them. Other times, when he wasn't feeling so kinky, he'd cum on my face, in my mouth, or on tits. He never shot off in a condom. After Devin fucked me silly, he came in my mouth.

******

I shook my head at Devin getting his lap dance. He was a cool dude. I think he was a midfielder for the Atlanta United soccer team. He used to pay me $3,000 every time we hooked up. Bet he didn't know I was out. I thought against going over to let him know that I was and continued my stride to the owner's office. I'd catch up with him later. When I got to the office door, I knocked and was told to enter.

"Aye, look who's made it home. Ms. Nikki Bunz. Good to see you, love."

"How you doin', Q? I see you still keep it poppin' twenty-four, seven 'round here." Q came from around his desk, giving me a warm hug.

"How long you been out?" he asked. Q was the coolest boss man in the world. He was a certified pimp, minus the suits, cane, and all the extra shit that comes along with the average pimp. One thing I liked about him was that he didn't let any of the girls at the club use any drugs. Weed was about it. No cocaine, meth, ice, pills, or any hard or addictive drugs were allowed for recreational use if you wanted to work for him. He even required that all the girls take a drug test twice a month. If you had a problem with it, then there was the door, was his motto. his club was not getting any bad publicity. Q respected a hustler. He knew the girls sold pussy in the private rooms. He collected his ten percent of the cut faithfully every time a room was used. He ran his business with an iron fist and no other strip club in the city could compete with him. Sorry Magic City, no disrespect, but it is what it is.

Just like I expected, Q gave me my job back with no hesitation. He let me decide when I wanted to work. Without a doubt, I chose the night shift on Thursday's, Friday's, Saturday's, and Sunday's. That was when the big bucks, no whammies were in the building. He agreed to my terms and as I was walking out, he reminded me of something.

"I see Nikki still got the Bunz."

"And you know this!" I laughed and did a five second twerk before walking out of his office.

Q was a trip. That was my boy, though. We had sex three times and I had to admit, he had some good dick. Despite this, he had to pay to play all three times. Boss man or not, my boy or not, Nikki Bunz treated no one differently when it came to business. I know some of you are curious as to how I ended up becoming a part of this life. Everyone has a backstory. Allow me the opportunity to catch you up to speed on mine.

Zion

Chapter Five

I was born on December 26th, 1992, in Jackson, Mississippi. It was the state's capital, but make no mistake about it, you can lose your life quick in that mothafucka. It seemed like there was a murder committed every five minutes. I was surprised the TV show, *The First 48* hadn't come to film a season or two. It's a city of survival of the fittest. Look at how we refer to the city; Jack-Town. Or how we name out each letter of our city. Jacking All Cowards Keepin' Suckas On Noid. Some city, huh? Fortunately for me, I wasn't raised in the streets of Jackson. I only dabbed in them whenever I was feeling adventurous or on one of my rebellious streaks. I came from a home where both my parents owned their own businesses. My father built one hundred to two hundred thousand dollars subdivision houses. My mother owned a tanning salon and sold clothes, shoes, and other accessories. We lived in the Woodleaf Subdivision in a $250,000 home. I was the second oldest of three siblings. We all went to a private school named, Jackson Academy. It was mostly white students, but there were a few black kids that attended. Not many, unfortunately. I'm not going to sit here and lie like I didn't see the racism and bullying some of the white kids were on, because I did see it. And my heart always went out to the victims. "They" say all white people are racists. That was a damn lie! I had never been prejudiced against any ethnic group. My parents didn't raise me to be that way. My family didn't have any hate towards anyone, no matter the color of their skin. I saw people the same way I saw myself, as a human being.

One day while in my freshman year, I got sick and tired of watching three white girls bullying this black girl. I stepped in and went to war for her. She and I both got our asses kicked, but we let them bitches know that enough was enough. We all got suspended, but in the end, I had a new friend, and her name was Sophia. She was originally from Texas and was an only child. Come to find out, we lived in the same neighborhood. Her dad was a retired ex-professional football player who'd played fifteen years in the NFL. He played seven years for the Dallas Cowboys, finishing his career with the New Orleans Saints. After the Saints released him, her dad decided to retire. A year later, he was offered a coaching job at Jackson State University. That's how they ended up in Mississippi.

Sophia and I became glued to the hip. We were always together. My white friends got jealous of her and stopped hanging with me altogether. I didn't care. They were too bougie for me anyway. I liked Sophia. Our parents became friends through us. Turns out, my dad knew all about Sophia's dad. My dad was a big Dallas Cowboys fan. Sophia and I spent a lot of nights and weekends at each other's homes. We talked about everything. When I used to talk about boys and who my latest crush was, Sophia would always get quiet. I'm talking every single time. One night I was staying over, we were in her bedroom, she finally confessed that she was more attracted to girls. She said she liked boys, but they just didn't make her heart flutter the way girls did. She said she didn't want her confession to upset me or make me want to end our friendship. I could care less if she was bi-curious or straight up gay. It didn't matter one way or the other, she was my friend. I had no judgement of her. I told her my feelings toward the subject, ensuring her that we would always be friends. I was struck in awe just a little when she asked me how I felt about girls. I had a real good feeling where she was going with the conversation. Despite my acumen, I said that I thought girls were pretty, but I'd never looked at one in a sexual way.

"Would you consider being with one if ever approached in that way?"

I thought it over before answering. "Honestly, I don't know. Why are you asking?" I quizzed, putting the pressure back on her.

"No reason," she said.

Imagine that very night, I woke up to her eating me out. Just as I was about to protest, I felt something I'd never felt in my entire life. The reason being, I was a virgin. I'd never even masturbated before. The closest I'd ever come to sex was kissing a few boys at school. That was it. What Sophia did to me that night changed my life entirely. She had me feeling like a junkie chasing after their first high. Every chance we got, I had her going down on me. The day she made me eat her out, I became a junkie to her taste. Sophia most certainly turned me out. I guess one could say we were a couple. We acted like one in private, but in front of our families, we hid in the closet. We were exceptionally good in keeping appearances. Even when we made it to our senior year, nobody knew about us. We weren't comfortable with telling them.

Speaking of my senior year in high school, Sophia's dad got another coaching job at the University of Texas as a special team's coach. They ended up moving to Austin, Texas. Sophia and I stayed in touch for a while, but eventually our friendship faded away.

I started hanging with my cousin, Rachel more. She was a month older than me. She was blonde with ocean blue eyes, tall and skinny like a model. I on the other hand, was a true redhead with green eyes, short with a booty that's rarely seen on a white girl. Rachel used to love to grab it, smack it, feel on it, pinch it, whatever she could to tease me about it. She'd seen more than her fair share of big booties. All she used to say was, "You gotta ass like a black girl." She went to

Calloway, a public school in the city. Another thing she used to make fun of me about is my name. I hated my name. Karolina Elizabeth Musgraves. How the hell you name a 90's baby some shit like that? Shame on my mother.

Anyway, the first time Rachel wanted me to hang out with her and her friends, she told me I had to change my name. "Are you kiddin' me?!" I asked, beyond shocked.

"No, I'm not kiddin' with you. I'm dead ass. I'm not takin' you anywhere near them with a name like that. I'm the only one who can joke you about your name."

"Is that supposed to make me feel any better? Because it's not."

"How about we go with the name, Nikki?" she said, spelling out my new name.

"Fine, whatever." I pretended to be mad, but in all actuality, I liked my new name. I adopted it from that point on. I had everybody calling me, Nikki, including my parents.

Fucking with Rachel is how I met my first black boyfriend. I was eighteen at the time. His name was Money. He was three years older than me. This was where my life really changed. I'd had my coochie ate, ate some coochie, and been fucked by an eight-inch dildo Sophia had purchased from a sex shop. All of that was fine and dandy. Why ain't nobody tell me how phenomenal, marvelous, remarkable, and outstanding the real deal would feel?

Mmm...mmngh...mmngh! My boyfriend's prodigious black cock had a bitch climbing the walls like a damn spider, wanting to turn backflips, spin on my head like a break-dancer. Anything that I've never done before, I was more than willing to do. I was hooked and there was no turning back for me. I fell head over heels in love with him. I began sneaking out of the house to be with him. Skipping school so we could spend a whole day fucking. I spent all my allowance on him.

I even stole from my parents to give to him if and when he needed it. I would do anything if he asked of me. I was so naive when it came to him, that he could've told me he was God, and my simple-minded ass would've believed him. He taught me so much about love, sex, and the game of life. He used to have me around his friends a lot. Sometimes Rachel would be with us and we would all be at Money's house having one big orgy. Other times, I'd be by myself. One day it was just me, Money, and five of his friends just hanging out. They were smoking weed and popping pills. I wasn't into the drugs. It had never been an interest for me. To each his own though.

That day, Money had me wear some booty shorts and he kept making me do little small things like, dump the ashtray, get some water for them, or go get something from his room for him. I saw the way his friends were peering at me. Their eyes were consumed with raging desire. Money pulled me into his room and told me that all five of his friends were willing to pay me $200 a piece to have sex with me. He said he'd split the money if I did since he was the one orchestrating the deal. Give it up to him, because he'd talked me into doing something that would prove my undying love to him. The unbelievable part, it felt fucking amazing to have a train ran on me. I've never felt so powerful lying there on my back or on my hands and knees, getting dicked down by a bunch of black men. I came over and over and over again. I didn't want to stop cumming. Afterwards, Money split the thousand dollars with me 50/50 like he said he would. We did this routine a few more times with different men. Three to four times with these two dykes. Old or young, they were paying to have sex with the redhead white girl with the phat ass. It was all good up until Money started withholding my cut. He had it in his mind that he was going to be my pimp and I would be his full-time whore. Not! I had way more sense than that. I loved him and all, in spite of, I was nobody's fool, no matter how naive I seemed at times. I knew I carried the bread and the butter between my legs. If anybody was going to pimp me out, it was going to be me and no one else but me.

Money got in his feelings when I confronted him about my pay and told him I wasn't going to be his slut bucket anymore and he beat my ass like I was a damn man. He dumped me on the side of the road, leaving me for dead. Luckily, I was found by one of Rachel's friends who took me to the hospital. I'd suffered a concussion, four broken ribs, a broken arm, and I had to have oral surgery on account of Money having kicked my teeth out. Every last one of them. My lips required stitches. JPD asked me if I knew my attacker and I lied like I didn't. I lied to my parents, to Rachel, to everybody who asked me who did me this way. I was hurt and shameful the way Money had done me. When my mother held a mirror in front of me, I sobbed uncontrollably. I stayed in the hospital almost a month. One day, Rachel came to visit and brought a visitor with her. It was the guy who'd found me. Tears streamed-rolled from my eyes. I couldn't thank him enough for his act of kindness and bravery. This man could have minded his own business and left me there to die, especially with me being a white girl, but he didn't. I would forever be grateful for him saving my life. When I was discharged from the hospital, he and I became good friends. Through my recovery, we talked almost every day. A few weeks after I'd made a full recovery, he was sent to prison and I never heard from him again.

After the whole experience with Money, I humbled myself. I went on to graduate just to make my parents proud. Afterall, I'd taken them through hell and back. They never gave up on me, believing that I still had a bright future awaiting me. Despite me graduating high school, I had no plans of going to college. Why, you might ask. Because I'd discovered that a gold mine rested between my legs. The plan I had would be the best of both worlds to me. I would get paid and would bust good nuts all in one. All I had to do was find some horny, rich, and wealthy clients and play out their ultimate sexual fantasies for them. So, what did I do? A year after graduating, I followed Rachel to Atlanta. She'd moved there with her dad after she caught her boyfriend cheating on her with her own mother. Drama. Can't live with it, can't live without it.

Zion

Chapter Six

"Freak hoes. Freak hoes. Bounce dat ass and make yo' knees touch yo' elbows."

Blaring from the club's speakers was Future rapping his strip club anthem, *Freak Hoes*. For this packed Friday night, I'd made it my performance song, as I followed Future's instructions to the T. Only, I added a little of my imagination to spice things up some. I spread my legs wide, bent over with my bare pussy on full display, and made my ass bounce in tune with the beat. When Future started rapping his verse, I dropped down on my hands and knees, letting my booty do a shimmy. I started rocking back and forth as if I was throwing it back to a long, fat cock. I stopped suddenly, making my right butt cheek do a dance of its own. Then my left one. Then both of them together. The horny crowd of men and women sounded off in cheers, throwing money onto the stage. I turned over on my back, holding my bare breasts as I made them jiggle. I opened my mouth, holding out my tongue, as I teased the many spectators like I was about to lick one of my nipples. This drove them crazier. All the while, my closed legs hung in the air, pussy playing peek-a-boo with my fans. I opened my legs. Closed them. Opened them again. I pulled my knees to my chest. For those close enough, they could see my pussy fluctuating. I made it move in rhythm with the song. the crowd cheered like they'd never seen such a thing before. I kept doing it. More cheers. More roars. More applauding. More money thrown onto the stage. I grabbed some and rubbed it all over my double-D's and stomach. Immediately upon the start of the chorus, I jumped to my feet, and made my knees touch my elbows all over again.

This was my first night back at the club. I didn't get the premiere spot like I was hoping I would. Q told me he wasn't giving me anything. If I wanted it, I had to work hard to get it. I had no problem doing that. Anything can be done as long as you have your mind set on doing. After the song ended, I gathered my money, thong, and bra, then went straight to my locker to stash my money. I'd count it later. Right now, I had more to get. I put on another thong and bra set and walked back out to see who wanted a lap dance or their own private show. I needed to hit the V.I.P. That was where the real money was at. So far, it was occupied with girls who'd been invited. I saw this black dude sitting at a table alone and was making my way over when I was stopped short by a fairly handsome one.

"Look at the redheaded, Kylie Jenner," he said with a smile.

"The name's Nikki Bunz," I said with indifference.

"Sorry, I didn't mean no harm, Love. Can I make it up to you by inviting you to my table for a lap dance?"

I looked him up and down. He had that dope boy kinda attire. I hated dope boys. They were so fuckin' arrogant, like the world belonged to them. Despite my assumptions of this dude, I needed the money, so what the hell. I went to his table where he had three other dudes sitting with him. They each had a dancer entertaining them. I told dude my price and he pulled out a bankroll as thick as my arm with nothing but them blue-faced hundreds. He made it his business to let me see before peeling off a couple of them to pay me. We had to wait until the next song before I started. In the meantime, he wanted me to sit down with him. He took that as an invitation to introduce himself.

"My name's Ro."

"Okay."

"You know the rapper, Lil' B?" he asked.

"Who doesn't know him? I thought he didn't rap anymore. He only produces music and makes movies and shit like that." I said.

"He does."

"So, you are tellin' me this because of what?"

"He's my brother. He's comin' here in a week to pick out some girls to be in his next movie."

"So why hasn't Q mentioned any of this to me or to any of the girls for that matter?" I asked him, doubting his claim. I thought he was just another dude trying to stunt or whatever. He shrugged his shoulders at my question.

"I don't know why Q hasn't told you or any of y'all for dat matter," He smiled. "Guess he hasn't gotten around to mentioning it to y'all. When you get a chance to, ask him. He'll tell you. I'm tellin' the truth. I'm here scoping' out the club because we're goin' to shoot a scene here."

"Oh, yea?" I had a different attitude now. For some strange reason, Ro didn't look like a dope boy anymore. He looked more like a businessman. I knew a lot about Lil' B from the articles I'd read on him while I was in prison. He was from Columbus, Mississippi, which was about two hours from where I was born. Lil' B had done time before for some straight up bullshit, I thought. I admired and respected how he took a few hundred dollars and turned them into millions. He'd made himself a platinum selling rapper. He'd won multiple Grammys BET, Soul Train, MTV, Billboards, and Video Music awards in his career. He was still active on the music scene. His rap group ISM was more in the spotlight than him. He produced my favorite R&B singer who had also won a plethora of awards herself. Lil' B was more into getting his Tyler Perry on. He'd produced a few movies that went straight to DVD and Netflix. Only one of his movies had made it to theaters. He said he was grateful for that. He made guest appearances in each of his movies if he wasn't the star in it already. Hearing that he was coming to the club, I saw opportunity although I had never acted a day in my life. Perhaps, I would get to star or co-star in a movie of his. I asked Ro what the movie was going to be about.

"His life. He's talked about it in interviews before. But now, he wants people to see his struggle and survival. It's goin' to be lit, real talk."

"Is he goin' to play himself or have someone else to do it?"

"He's undecided at the moment."

"Mm-kay. Well, this song is about to end. You ready for your lap dance?"

"Ready when you are."

Usher's *No Limit* came on just as I stood up. I put a knee in between Ro's legs to spread them and turned around to put my ass all in his face. I looked over my shoulder to see the fire in his eyes. "Damn," I could read his lips as he gawked and lusted after all that booty before him. He lifted his eyes to mine. Even a blind man could see that Ro wanted to fuck me. I made my ass bounce, drawing his attention back to there. I shook it from left to right. He had to restrain himself from touching me. By the time I sat in his lap, he was as hard as steel. I could feel his hard on and could tell he packed a serious tool. I could feel that monster beneath me. I gyrated my hips, making my pussy rub back and forth over him. I leaned back, placing my head beside his.

"You fine as hell!" His breath was cool against my ear.

"You like a white girl with ass like mine?" I asked loud enough for him to hear me.

"Fuck yea! Love it!" He flexed his dick against my now wet pussy. I hated that our clothes prevented us from really feeling each other. It was the smell of him that was turning me the hell on. I loved a man that wore the perfect cologne.

"Can you feel how hard I am?" I nodded my head. "You like the way it feels?" Again, I nodded as I ground down hard on him, his hips started to move with mine.

Were we hunchin'? Oh, God, say it ain't so!

"Just know when you roll with a nigga like me, there's no limit baby!" Ro sang along with Usher. I let out a soft whimper. Maybe I was just horny because I still hadn't gotten a piece of dick since I'd been home. I raised up, positioning myself so that my clit could grind against him. His dick stood up in the perfect angle. I couldn't believe what my freaky ass was about to do. Some things are just too good to disregard. I rocked back and forth fast. Grinded hard. Harder even. I had to time it right, the song was about to end. Faster. Faster. One more second. God, yes! My body shook like a seizure, I came so hard. I couldn't disguise what I'd just done.

"Bitch! Ain't no way you just bust a whole nut dancin' on this man?!" One of the dancers who was dancing for Ro's friends called me out. I was a bit embarrassed, but I still told the truth. It didn't faze Ro at all. He wanted to pay for another lap dance. He gave me $500 this time. The guys I thought were his friends turned out to be his brother and two cousins. I ended up giving them lap dances. After seeing what I brought to the table, they dismissed the other girls. Them hoes was mad as fuck. I'd collected $1,400 just from lap dances. I asked Ro would he like a private show. I was going to fuck him if he said yes. Unfortunately, he had business to attend to first thing in the morning. Be that as it may, he gave me his number and told me to call. I asked him if he would be with his brother when he came to the club.

"Yes, I'll be with him."

"Put in a good word for me?"

"I gotcha, Kylie Jenner," He laughed. I didn't. I hated when people compared me to her. I was prettier than her and my ass was way fatter, not to mention, mine was real. I frowned at Ro. "You know I'm just messin' with you, Nikki Bunz. Hit me up to remind me about puttin' in a good word for you."

"I most certainly will."

They left and I went to take a shower. After that, I went straight to Q's office to find out if Lil' B was indeed shooting a scene of his movie here. Q confirmed it. He said he was going to tell me, but hadn't had the time to. Without a doubt, it was time for me to put on my game face. This was one opportunity I couldn't let slip out of my hands. Little did the girls know, I had the advantage over them. I had a number. A number I would be calling in the next few days to secure my spot in the movie. When favorable circumstances knock at your door, I learned to open the door wide to let it in.

Chapter Seven

"Hey is this, Ro?"

"Yea. Who dis?"

"This Nikki from the club the other night."

"Ah, my Kyl-"

"You better not, or I'ma hang this phone up on you," We both started laughing. I'd finally decided to give him a call. I know I said I would make him wait two days, but I waited three because I had to work Sunday night. Since it was my day off, it was the right time to call.

"So, what's up, Ms. Nikki Bunz? How's your day goin' so far?"

"It's goin'. I'm just relaxin' in bed at the moment. I haven't called you at the wrong time, have I?"

"Nah, you're good. I'm not in bed but I'm just coolin'."

"Where's your better half?" I asked, wondering did he have one.

"Who? My ol' lady?"

"Yea."

"Probably out shoppin' knowin' her. Where's yours?"

"Probably somewhere waitin' to meet my fine ass," That made him laugh.

"I'm sure he's out there waiting to meet you like you said."

"To be honest, I don't have time for a man. I'm on my grind right now. Gotta get this money," I said with backbone.

"I feel you on dat. If you don't mind me asking, how old are you?"

"Twenty-four, soon to be twenty-five. Is Ro your real name?"

"Roshawn's my middle name. Joniel's my first name. What's yours?"

"Oh, hell nah! I'm not tellin' you."

"Why not? I just told you mine."

"Because you're gonna laugh at me. Nope. No indeed. Not gonna tell you," I said, laughing.

"I'm not gonna laugh."

"A lie! You're already laughin', and I haven't even told you yet."

"That's because you're makin' me laugh," We laughed for a few seconds. It felt good to be having a real and authentic laugh, especially one with a man. I didn't want to get too personal with Ro. We still had business to discuss. He ended up beating me to the conversation.

"So, did you get up with Q and ask him about me?"

"Yea. You one hunnid. When are y'all supposed to come again? I wanna make sure I'm ready when y'all do."

"Nikki, stop the madness. You know damn well you already ready."

"How do you know me so well?" More laughter. I was starting to like him the more we talked. "Let me ask you somethin'," I said.

"Go ahead."

"What kinda girls do you think your brother is goin' to be lookin' for?"

"To be real witcha, I approached you for a specific reason. You're special and you don't even know it. You'll see."

"What's that supposed to mean?" I asked with an intense desire to know. He had my undivided attention talking like that.

"I'll just let you see for yourself. All you gotta do is be there."

"Trust and believe, I'll be there." I promised.

"Now, can we discuss the private show you owe me?" he asked.

"Funny, I don't recall me owing you one. I only remember offerin' you one." I said, making him laugh.

"Is the offer still on the table?"

"All you gotta do is show up."

"Don't you know baby. Yeah, I'll be there! I'll be there! Just call my name, and I'll be there," This dude started singing the Jackson 5 song, causing me to double over in laughter. Ro was crazy. We talked for another thirty minutes or so, just getting to know each other a little. I asked him if he was a rapper. He said he was more of a talent scout for the label. The last time I interacted with a so-called talent scout, I ended up going to prison. Before I hung up the phone, Ro told me to hold on before I did.

"What's your name?"

"I'm still not tellin' you, Joniel Roshawn. Bye!" I hung up on him, laughing my ass off.

It felt great talking to him. I was still curious about what he meant when he said I was special and all. I wanted to write it off as he was spittin' game, but he had a serious tone, which made me sort of believe him. There was a knock at my door and in walked Tia, asking me why I was smiling the way that I was. She came and sat on the bed with me. I still hadn't told her about Lil' B coming to visit the club and his reason for coming. It wasn't like she still danced there.

Tia was the proud side piece of a very wealthy celebrity who was married with three kids. Everyone who watched TV or movies knew the actor Evan Smith. He made his acting debut when he was thirteen. He'd been a child star with a record-breaking TV show on the Disney Channel earning him one of the top three child stars on TV. By the age of twenty, he'd made his way onto the big screen working in action and comedy films. From the age of twenty to age thirty-seven, he'd starred in over forty blockbuster films. Evan had won only one Oscar in his long career, but as a child, he'd won dozens of People's Choice Awards. Tia had met him one night she'd danced for him. They got to know each other mentally, physically, and spiritually. You name it. They fell in love with each other. After that, he wanted her all to himself. He told her he would take care of her if she stopped stripping. She did. He kept it all the way real with her about what his intentions of her were. He wasn't leaving his family and he expected Tia to never ask him to. The moment she did, he would cut her off. Although he had to keep her a secret from his wife and the public's eye, Evan loved Tia. She went along with it by being the best "other woman" she could be. By playing by the rules, she was able to live in this two-bedroom condo and drive a 2017 BMW Coupe. Mind you, we're in 2017. Each year, she would get an upgrade as long as it was a BMW. She didn't care about titles on relationships or nothing of the sort. She didn't care if Evan loved her or not like he professed he did. Tia was a hustler, yesterday, today, and tomorrow. She would forever be one. I learned so much from her.

She asked me what I had planned for tonight because Evan would be in town later and he was coming over. She wanted to make sure they would be alone. Although she'd told him about me, Evan and I hadn't met yet. She wanted to wait until tomorrow to introduce us. I told her I was going to dance at a bachelor's party with Shamarah and probably wouldn't be home until late in the morning.

"Good. I'm about to fuck Evan like he's never been fucked before," She boasted.

"I thought that happened the last time y'all got it in?" I giggled.

"My point exactly." she laughed. I went on to tell her about Lil' B and my conversation with Ro.

"You can turn this into a real opportunity for you, Nikki. Lil' B's certified. He's about his business. All you gotta do is be about yours. You're goin' to fuck his brother, aren't you?" she wanted to know.

"I don't know. Haven't really thought about it," I lied. By all means I had. Particularly, before Tia had walked in.

"If it gets you in the movie, you better. I want to see you in it. That way, I'll have a part time man as a movie star and a best friend as one. Can't go wrong with connections like those."

"Aww!" I said. She had touched my emotions with that comment. "I gotta get ready to start my day. Got to go get this pretty pussy a Brazilian wax before I sit it on Evan's mustache."

"Ewww! Don't you think that's T-M-I?" I've seen Tia naked a thousand times. I've only thought about her in a sexual way once. I looked at her like a sister, so I didn't want to think about what she was or wasn't doing in the bedroom.

"Be careful at the bachelor party. You know how they can get out of hand sometimes." She said, always concerned about my safety.

"I will," I promised. She kissed me on my forehead and walked out of my room. Moments later, I got a text from Ro.

Ro: Is your name Emma Jean? Patti Mae? Gertrude? He even left three laughing face emojis.

This dude was really funny. I laughed hard before sending him a reply with the middle finger, the shit turd, and laughing faces with the tears emojis.

Me: Keep guessing.

On that note, I got out of bed to start my day.

******

Shamarah's punk ass could've told me we were dancing for a bunch of lesbians. Her weak ass couldn't say shit when I cussed her out in one of the bedrooms of the mansion these bitches rented out for tonight. I wasn't mad that I was stripping for some women, I did a lot of that at the club. Besides, I'd had sex with a number of females before. I was only feeling some type of way because Shamarah was supposed to tell me what I was walking into. She knew I hated walking blindly into something. It made me feel like I was a sitting duck, all vulnerable and shit. Well, since I was here now, I might as well get the show on the road. It was me, Shamarah, and four other girls from the club. While we were changing into our outfits, Shamarah gave me the full rundown on who we were dancing for. The girl getting married was a professional basketball player in the WNBA, who played for the Atlanta Dream. She had a few of her teammates, family members, and friends here. It was about twenty-five of them in all.

We all walked out there and Shamarah showed me the one who was getting married. She was tall, not like a man though, she was cute, but you could tell she was a butch. I was looking around the room and there were some pretty ladies in attendance, all looking drunk, high, and horny. They were turning up their cups and smoking their blunts, watching us make our way to where we were going to dance at. I heard a few of them making comments.

"These hoes bad!"

"Look at the asses on these bitches!"

"I like the red-bone with the tattoos!"

"I like the one with the gold dreads!"

"Look at the ass on the white bitch! Don't nobody touch her. She's mine!" That last comment came from the one getting married. I didn't know whether to call her the bride or groom. I didn't know how to classify it. Needless to say, she handcuffed me. Not literally. She wasn't letting me out of her sight. Women are worse than men when they're drunk or high and got a naked woman in front of them. They couldn't keep their damn hands to themselves. Nevertheless, the music started and so did we. The agreement was for us to dance for two hours. In that time span, I had made $2,000. The girl getting married, who I decided call Butch, offered to pay us for an extra hour. We all agreed to stay. Butch made sure no one touched me, but her and one of her teammates. Her teammate wasn't all butch like her. In fact, she had sex appeal and a face I could appreciate. I loved her long silky black hair and tattoos. I got naked again and popped, locked, and dropped it for them some more. I took turns giving them lap dances. Time and time again, I had to keep pulling their fingers out of my pussy. Horny bitches! I suppressed my anger on the strength that they kept the cash flowing.

It was getting close to the last hour and I knew they were going to offer me money to have sex with them because of the orgy taking place before us. All of the other dancers, including Shamarah, were getting their pussies ate or they were busy eating pussy themselves. I looked at Shamarah as she rode a bitch's face. She winked at me when we made eye contact, then blew me a kiss before closing her eyes to return to her pleasure. One girl was bent over a chair with her knees on the arms of it getting ate out from the back by the prettiest girl in the room. One girl was lying on her back with a head between her legs and a pussy riding her face. Another was riding some bitch's face while a bitch sucked on her nipples. The other girl was nowhere to be found. I wondered if she left. I don't know how much money they were all being paid, but I was about to raise the ante. Since these bitches wanted to run a train on me, I was about to run up a check. I had them right where I wanted them. So much that they offered me $5,000. In addition to the

$2,000 I had already pocketed, how could I not let these hoes taste my vanilla treat?

They wanted to take a shower first. I thought they would put it down on me in the shower, but they had other plans with me. They did clean me up good though. Afterwards, they led me to one of the bedrooms where my money was sitting on the king-sized bed. I grabbed it and with my other money, I put it in the drawer until we were done. They excused themselves and when they came back into the room, both of them were naked, wearing big black strap-ons. Wow! They'd planned ahead, I see. Real shit, I was excited!

"How big are they?" I asked, staring at the strap-ons.

"Nine inches," The pretty one answered. I named her Pretty Girl. She was fine with a nice round and firm ass with C-cup titties. Her nipples were pierced. Her pretty brown skin was intact. Butch however, she was alright. She had a nice booty, flat stomach, small breasts though. I bit my bottom lip, ready for some action as laid back, spreading my legs wide for them. Pretty Girl was the first to crawl between them.

"A real redhead, I see," she whispered before kissing my pussy lips like they were the pair on my face. She kissed them again. And again. Finally, she ran the tip of her tongue up and down the cleft of my vagina, sending shockwaves straight to my clit. Butch got into bed, positioning herself by my head, her strap-on poking me in the face. I looked up. "Suck it," she said. *Oh, what the hell,* I thought. I parted my mouth and began sucking on the dildo. Not long into it, this bitch starts moaning and shit like she has a real dick and could feel my warm, wet mouth. I swear to God, I almost busted out laughing at her ass. She even had the nerve to hold her head back with her mouth hung open. No, she didn't! Just too much! I was glad Pretty Girl made me turn my attention back to her. My tender pearl had to be her favorite meal the way she was sucking on it. She grabbed my ass with both hands, lifting it off the bed and ate all the pussy she could as Butch fucked my mouth, stifling my moans with her rubber cock. She was squeezing my breasts and pinching my nipples. How the hell did she know I loved having my nipples pinched? Butch pulled away shortly thereafter.

"Spit on it," I spit all over that motherfucker, shining it up real good. I was just as turned on as she was at this point. "That's right, get it wet 'cause I'm 'bout to fuck you good and hard with it,"

"Mmmmmm, are you, baby?" I teased.

"Come sit on this dick." We repositioned ourselves so I could ride her fake dick. It took a while to fit fully inside of me because I was so tight. Don't forget that this is my first sexual encounter since I've been out. I rocked slowly on it, letting it stretch me. I could feel it all in my stomach. "Ssss. Shhh. Shhhh. Shhiittt! Ooouuu-fuuu-fuuu-fuuuuucckkkk!" I moved my ass up and down, gripping the dildo with my muscles. "Mmmnggghhh!"

Butch began sucking my nipples at the same time Pretty Girl's tongue pressed against my backdoor. What they were doing to me felt incredible. Pretty Girl made me hold still so she could slide her tongue in my ass.

"Fuck! Fuck! Fuck!" I reached back, pulling her head, needing her tongue to go further up my butt. She flattened her tongue, somehow, she managed to wiggle it inside of me. I screamed, "So fuckin' nasty! Oh my God! You're so fuckin' nasty! I love it! Eat my ass! Oooouuuu-fuck!" Butch kept drilling me from below, tapping my pussy in the right spot. "Ohhh! Ohhh! Ohhh, my goodness I'm about to cummmm! Unghhh! Make me cum baby! Oooouuuu, make me cummmmmm!" It wasn't long before I was cumming all over the plastic.

Pretty Girl wanted me to jump off the cock so she could suck my cum from the dildo. I couldn't resist getting behind her to eat her out while she had that round, juicy booty sticking in the air. It was difficult getting to her due to the strap being in the way. I made it work. We ended up with me riding Butch some more. That's the way they wanted it. A few minutes into it, Pretty Girl began applying K-Y to my ass. I looked over my shoulder watching her insert a finger into my tight hole. Not long after, she added a second one, getting me primed and ready for what she was about to do to me. I kept my eyes on her as she slid the plum-shaped head of her strap-on into my tight ass. Instinctively, I tensed up because I've never been double penetrated before. Pretty Girl encouraged me to relax. I heeded her advice to accommodate the head of the swollen dildo as she stayed still, allowing me to become accustomed to this new sensation. I could feel the excitement pulsing in my clit. With a firm hold on my hips, she began rocking back and forth, slowly working more and more of the giant dildo in my ass. When she felt that I was sufficiently relaxed, she quickened her pace, pulling firmly on my hips as she pushed forward to bury herself to the root in my butt. A growl of pure satisfaction came from my lips.

"Urrgghhh! Ahhhhhh! Ahhhhhhh! That's how you feel about my ass? Just gon' fuck it like that, huh? Just gon' make a bitch feel soooo good-goooood! Ungh, harder! Fuck it harder!"

Pretty Girl did as I said as I clamped my muscles down on the dildo in my pussy. Every cell in my body screamed in pleasure. "My a-ass and pu-pussy! Being fucked at the same time feels so good! Yesss! Yesss! Whoooo-yesssss!"

After I said that, I went to speaking in tongues. I've never felt pleasure like this. I came so hard. A bitch was ready to go to sleep sucking on my thumb now. I thought they were done, but they weren't. Pretty Girl pulled out of my ass making a popping sound, then took off her strap-on, and went to pull up a chair to sit in. She made me crawl over to her all while Butch was smacking me on the ass calling me a fine ass white bitch. I went straight to Pretty Girl's meaty pussy and wrapped my lips around her clitoris. I was making her body shake when Butch entered my ass and began pounding away.

"Fuck you doing with all this ass, huh?" She buried the dildo to the hilt, moving her body from left to right. I stopped eating Pretty Girl to entertain Butch.

"It's for you to fuck like you please. You're gonna talk or are you gonna fuck my ass harder, bitch? You know that's what we both want. For you to-ooooooouuuuuuu-fuuccckkkkk! Yesssssss!"

Butch was giving it to me the way I'd told her to give it to me. "Pull my hair!" I demanded. She grabbed a fistful of my hair and fucked my ass hard the way I loved it. I tried eating Pretty Girl some more but the pleasure of getting my ass pounded was too much and I came again. I really thought they were done with me now. However, they had more plans for me. They were making me work for them five bands. Pretty Girl put her strap-on back on and made me sit down on her reverse cowgirl. "Ungh-ungh. Put it in your ass." She said when she saw me sitting my pussy on the strap-on. As soon as it was buried deep, Butch came and entered my pussy. I'd gotten what I bargained for. They fucked me completely. What a way to get fucked for my first time since being home. These bitches were the truth.

Come to find out, they were marrying each other. I was happy for them. They'd definitely made me a happy woman. Kudos to them. To be fucked like they fucked me was historic. I would never forget them. Butch told me she had a birthday party coming up next month and invited me to come. They were willing to pay for my services again. I couldn't turn their offer down. I told them we could get together again. I gathered my things and went to find Shamarah and the girls. Every last one of them was knocked the fuck out. I woke them up and we left. I checked my phone and had a message from Ro.

Ro: *Goodnight, Billie Jean.*

He left a smiley face emoji beside it. I smiled and pressed start on my Camaro.

Chapter Eight

I swear I didn't want to wake up. After a hot shower, I'd probably been asleep no more than an hour. I was exhausted from the many orgasms I had earlier and needed some rest. I just wish my bladder had gotten the memo. It wanted my ass sitting on a toilet, or it was going to release itself in my bed. I kicked the covers off- me, mad at myself for having to pee this bad, and got up to use the bathroom. I wasn't fully awake. Semi sleepwalking was the better term. All I know is that I was ready to get this over with and get back in bed.

I pushed the door open and there Evan stood booty butthole naked with his dick in hand, pissing. I was fully awake now. In the two seconds all of this had gone down, he and I made eye contact.

"Hey," He smirked and kept about his business.

I was so embarrassed walking away from the door as quickly as I could. How could I forget that he was there? I'm so damn stupid! On top of that, I was only wearing panties, so he got a full visual examination of my breasts. I knew that was the reason his ass smirked the way he did. I went to put on my clothes like I was on the run from the police and they were seconds from kicking down my door. My heart was beating rapidly. I cracked the door, peeping out to see Evan's naked ass going back to his and Tia's room, closing the door behind him. The coast was clear. I went back to the bathroom to relieve myself, the image of Evan still in my mind. He was more handsome in person. His impeccable chest. His note-perfect abs. He definitely spent a lot of hours in the gym.

"Stop!" I screamed in my head. "Please don't do this to me!" I tried reasoning with my formation of mental objects. Even flaccid, Evan's dick was big and beautiful. I imagined it at full length. "Stop it, damn it!" Why were my thoughts betraying me? Tia was my best friend for crying out loud. I shook my head, trying to erase my thoughts. I forced myself to think of something else. My favorite food. My favorite heels. The gas mileage on my dashboard. Anything that would take my mind away from its current activity. There. All done. Time to go back to sleep. Before throwing the covers over my head, I looked at the 5:15 displayed on my phone. Geesh!

I didn't get back up until 12:30ish. I brushed my teeth and took another shower just to wake all the way up. I put on a pair of skinny jeans, a white wife beater, and my all white Air Force Ones. It was chillaxin' day for me. I walked slowly to the living room, hoping Evan was gone. To my disappointment, he was still here. Good thing he had on clothes this time around. My mind conjured up a picture of his huge dick, but I hurried up and dismissed that fast. He was in the kitchen with Tia making sandwiches for lunch. This dude had all the money and fame one could have and he's here enjoying a simple ham and cheese sandwich with the woman he loved. Well, one of them anyway. I really wish they'd gone to a fancy restaurant because I didn't want to be anywhere near Evan. Oh, the paparazzi. How could I forget.

"Hey, bitch. You finally decided to get up, huh?" Tia greeted me.

"Yea, I'm up. What's up with you? Hey, Evan." I really, and I do mean, really, didn't want to acknowledge Evan. Why me?

"You must be, Nikki? Pleasure to meet you. Tia's told me a lot about you," he said.

I avoided eye contact with him, still embarrassed from our first encounter. I wondered what he was thinking of me. The man had seen my boobs. Did he like them? Did he think that they were perfect? Oh God, stop it, Nikki.

"Pleasure to meet you as well. I'm sure you've heard nothin' but good things about me as I've heard nothin' but good things about you," I said.

"Good things like what?" Dang, I wasn't expecting him to ask me that.

"Just the way you treat my girl and how you make her feel at the end of the day. Nothin' too intimate though."

"Yea, I bet," he laughed. "So, what does she do when I'm not around?"

"Nothin'. She gets all dressed up just to watch Netflix."

"Loyal, I see,"

"Hellooo. Y'all not about to sit here and talk about me like I'm not even here," Tia cut in. "As a matter of fact, we're changin' the subject. Nikki, you want one of these sandwiches?" She giggled. I told her to fix me two. "Help yourself. My phone's ringing." She left to retrieve her phone from her bedroom.

"Don't worry about last night. It was an honest mistake, eh?" Evan broke the silence between us.

"Right," I said, grabbing the bread. "And I hope it never happens again."

"So, what do you do in your spare time?" he asked, making conversation now.

I played nice by responding, "I spend the majority of my time hustlin'."

"Hustling like how? I mean, if you don't mind me asking."

"Pass the mayo, please. I'm what Tia used to be before she met you. Unfortunately for me, I haven't met my Prince Charming to rescue me out of the trenches yet."

He was about to say something else when Tia returned. I finished making my sandwiches and we sat around eating, Tia and I listening to Evan tell his stories of some of the movies he's starred in. I told him about my potential appearance in Lil' B's movie. To my utter surprise, he and Lil' B were in talks about making a comedy movie right after Lil' B finished shooting the one about his life.

"You make that happen and we'll see about getting you a small role in our movie." Evan exclaimed. Opportunities after opportunities were lining themselves up in a straight line for me. Evan turned out to be cool. He was down to earth and had a sense a humor. I thought he would be stuck on himself, all egotistical, and arrogant. But he was the complete opposite. I finally stopped having images of him being naked. Finally! I stood to leave the lovebirds alone to do their thang when Tia pulled me to the side, saying that she was in the mood to give Evan some head. That was my queue to leave. I went over to Rachel's to see what she had going on. Before I got out of my car, I sent Ro a text.

Me: *WYD?*

By the time I walked inside of Rachel's apartment, he'd texted back.

Ro: *Still tryin' to figure out your name. Is it Claudia? 'Cause you look like a Claudia. LMAO!*

This dude here was way too funny with himself. He texted right back, saying he was about to drop his daughter off at home, and was about to chill after that. I asked him if I could chill with him. He said if I wanted to drive to Mississippi then I could. I texted back a sad face emoji with a follow up text saying maybe next time. I thought he lived somewhere in Atlanta. We went back and forth a few more messages then I told him I would talk to him later. To be honest, I was looking forward to meeting his brother. Mark my words, one day I'm going to be one of those people who'll be able to say, "I saw. I came. And I conquered!" I'ma shock the world one day!

Chapter Nine

It was an early Friday afternoon the day Lil' B and his entourage came to the club. Q had shut down the club so we could make this happen. If you let me tell it, Q was more excited to get the club's name on screen than us girls actually being in the movie. Most of us hadn't had that much sleep and I was one of them. Be that as it may, I was on my A-game, prepared to show Lil' B that I belonged in his movie. The top fifteen money makers of the club had two minutes each to dance ourselves onto the big screen. I was set to be the eleventh to perform. We weren't told how the judging would go. We were just told to give our best. All the girls were seated to the right of the stage, watching as Lil' B and his companions made their way to center stage to take their seats. I saw Ro and we both smiled. I looked at Lil' B and my heart fluttered. I thought Ro was astonishingly handsome. Lord, Lil' B's a remarkably beautiful man. He was short, around my height, sexy-hot, light-skinned with long braids, and had an aura that lit up the room when he walked in. You could see his confidence a mile away. I heard some of the girls commenting about him, saying some of the things I was thinking. Shamarah was sitting next to me goofing off with her remarks about Lil' B.

"I bet his lil short ass got a big dick," I couldn't help but laugh along with her and the girls that were in earshot.

"You know what they say, big things come in small packages. Too bad we'll never find that out," I said.

"Speak for yourself. Fuck around and let me get in this movie, I'll tell you all about it." Shamarah exclaimed.

"Bitch, please. You'll probably get in the movie, but you ain't fuckin' him." I countered.

"Bet somethin' then." We made a friendly wager of $100. It was now time to set the fun and games aside. It was time to handle business. The first girl was up.

Right before it was my turn, I looked over to Ro. He looked at me, then got Lil' B's attention, who looked at me as Ro whispered something in his ear. I didn't have time to decipher the whole meaning of it because I was up next. When the beat dropped, so did I. I wanted to get naked so bad for Lil' B. I wanted him to see my body. My double-D's. My pretty pink pussy. My voluptuous booty bouncing like a basketball for him. I wanted him to see me whole. To my disappointment, we were told to keep on our clothes. wondered if we would be nude in the movie. I was sure hoping so. I did leave little to the imagination. I wore the shortest shorts I owned and a halter top that showed my hard nipples sticking out. Guess what else? I didn't have on any panties. The gloves were off. I made sure they got a good view of my camel toe. I put it right in their faces for them to see. After my two minutes were up, Ro gave me a standing ovation. I blew him a kiss before looking at Lil' B. He had a nonchalant way of looking at me. I wish I could read his thoughts because he was now staring at me like recognition was setting in. I had to go. The next girl was up.

After every girl performed, Lil' B and Q walked away to talk. In the meantime, I was talking to Shamarah when Ro walked up.

"You did great, Love," he said.

"What about me? How did I do?" Shamarah asked before I had the chance to say thank you. Ro smiled that smile I was starting to grow on. "You did great, too." He said and I introduced them.

"So., did we get the part?" Shamarah was straightforward. I wanted to know as well.

"That's not on me to decide. But if it helps, I'll put in a word for you."

"Absolutely. You make sure you do that. Well, whatever it is that you two have goin' on, I'ma leave y'all to it. Nice to meet you. Nikki don't let this dude leave without us both havin' havin' roles. You got me?"

"I got you, babe." Shamarah walked over to where some of the other girls had gone.

"She's a trip."

"You don't know the half. That's my girl though. How have you been since we last talked?"

"Good. How about you?" he asked.

"No complaints."

"You're beautiful."

"Thanks," I blushed. I couldn't remember the last time someone called me that. All the men I had been with always commented on how phat my ass is, how juicy my titties were, how good and tight my pussy was, and how excellent I sucked dick.

"Would you like to sit down?" I asked Ro. We took a seat and talked a good ten minutes before Lil' B and Q came back. Lil' B had all of us to gather around so he could announce that he was using all of us in the movie. In spite of the fact, only five of us would really be seen. We wouldn't know who those five would be until the day they shot the scene here. I was cool with that. I still had the advantage over the girls. I was confident I would be one of the five chosen. Ro asked me if I wanted to hang out since he was in town for the next two days.

"Can I take a raincheck? I swear I want to. The thing is, I haven't had much sleep. I had to work last night and didn't get in until five this morning, then had to get right back up to come here. I'm runnin' on fumes and need to power up." I said honestly.

"I can understand dat. You need your beauty rest to make you even more beautiful."

"Awww! You're so sweet."

"I've been told dat a time or two. You workin' tonight?"

"I am."

"Cool. Do I get my private show tonight?"

"I still owe you that, don't I? Well, I don't owe you, but I got you." We laughed.

"Had to throw dat in there, didn't you? What time should I be here?"

"About the same as last time."

"Say no more. I'll see you then. Can I have a hug before I go?"

"Sure can." We stood to hug. He still smelled good. Made my pussy tingled. Down girl! Now is not the time!

That night, I didn't see him in the club. I looked around for him, but he was nowhere in sight. Guess he had to do a raincheck of his own. Oh well, I went about my business as usual, running my bands up. One of the security men told me I was wanted in private room number three. Ro had snuck in on me. I smiled and went straight there, waiting to turn him the hell on. He'd better brought condoms. I was about to ride that dick until he couldn't take it no more. I walked in, closing the door behind me, pussy jumping up and down in expectation. I turned around and gotdamn it, there was Evan sitting in a chair, dressed in a disguise with an ugly ass smug look on his face.

"What are you doin' here?" I yelled over the music, highly disappointed in seeing him here.

"I want a private lap dance from you, without the world knowing about it."

"You do know Tia's a part of the world, don't you?"

"Of course, I do,"

"Have you forgotten that she's my friend? Let me correct that for you, she's my best friend!" I yelled again, this time the music had nothing to do with it.

"Why are you screaming?"

"Tsk, because this is not right what you're tryin' to do, that's why."

"I get it. She's your best friend. I don't want to overstep my boundaries."

"I can't tell, 'cause you are…"

"Nikki, you left a lasting impression on me. I'm sure I'm not the only man you've had this effect on." He tried to use flattery, hoping I'd reconsider. I was having none of it.

"That's beside the point, Evan. I can't betray Tia like this."

"Like what? All you're doing is giving me a lap dance, which you're getting paid to do."

"This is not right. I can't do it," I said.

"Even if I give you whatever you ask for?" he tempted me.

"I'm sorry, I can't."

"$2,000?" I shook my head. "Three?" I still shook my head. "$5,000 is my final offer." Damn, he was putting major pressure on me.

What would Tia do if she were in this predicament, I thought. She'd get her money without compromising our friendship. $5,000 is a helluva lot of money to turn down just for a lap dance. "No touchin'." I finally gave in, but not before giving strict orders first. "You get two songs." I should've said only one, but since he was being so big-hearted, I thought I should show a little generosity myself.

He gave me the money in a small bag. He had on some black Nike sweatpants. I don't think he had any underwear on. Whew! This was going to be one of the hardest lap dances I ever had to give. Why? When I felt his dick getting hard, it was excessive in length, and it seemed like it wouldn't stop stretching. No! No! No! Don't do this! Think about Tia. The money. Anything but his hips swaying and my pussy grinding down on his hard cock. I swear that motherfucker was huge. He made it thump, making direct contact with my clit. I instantly jumped up, backing away from him.

"I'm sorry. I can't do this." I wanted to cry, feeling like I was giving the perfect exhibition of disloyalty. I started for the door.

"Wait-wait-wait!" Exclaimed Evan. "Just dance for me. You don't have to be in my lap. The money's still yours if you just dance."

I stopped, took a couple of deep breaths, and made a change in my direction. I could do what he was asking. I told him I wasn't getting naked, he said I didn't have to. Easy peasy. Let me make this money and get the hell out of here. I did exactly what he asked me. As soon as I was done, I got my money and walked out of there with no talk, no thank you, did you enjoy your dance, no nothing, but a whole lot of distance between us. I was hoping I'd never see Evan again.

I made it home around four, and to my amazement, Tia's bedroom door was wide open, and Tia was screaming Evan's name, encouraging him to keep fucking her in the fashion he was.

"Like this?" I heard him ask, followed by a smacking sound that I assumed was a slap on Tia's ass.

"Fuck yea! Slang that dick, Evan! Oooouuu-baby slang it! Ha-har-harder! Harder baby! Fuck me harder!"

Could Evan fuck her any harder than he already was? Evidently, he could. I could hear their skin slapping against each other. Here was the real question to all of this. Why were my feet still glued to the floor? I hadn't moved an inch. I heard

Tia ask him if he was about to cum. All I could hear was Evan mumbling, grunting, and breathing hard. In her best porn star imitation, Tia told him to cum all over her pretty face. There was a brief moment of silence. Soon after, "Ah shit!" Evan howled.

"Mmmm-hmmmm...Hell, yes. Cum so warm on my face." Tia murmured.

I imagined her gliding Evan's dickhead across her lips and face, rubbing it into her skin the way I would be doing. A moment passed and I heard slurping and smacking sounds. I knew exactly what Tia was doing. That's it, taste his seed. Was she sucking only the tip? Half of that big dick? Or did she have the whole thing buried in her throat? What did Evan's cum taste like? Sweet? Salty? I could still hear her slurping as my feet finally found the will to move.

I needed a shower. A cold one in fact. I was so horny, it hurt. In spite of that, I had to wait. The sex machines beat me to it. While waiting my turn, I fingered myself to a quiet orgasm. Somebody please remind me to invest in a vibrator because my pointer and middle fingers caught a damn cramp, almost fucking up my nut. Anyway, when I got out of the shower, I bust another nut before drifting off to la-la land.

Zion

Chapter Ten

"Evan, what the fuck!"

I jumped out of bed, titties bare, looking for a shirt to put on. I had to stop sleeping like this when he's here. This was getting old, super-fast. What was happening now, was on a much bigger scale than the bathroom incident. This son-of-a-bitch was in my room, in my damn bed, naked as the day he was born. On top of all of that, he'd been licking on my nipples. That's what woke me up. I considered that a major violation. Semi-rape if you asked me.

"You've lost your damn mind, haven't you!" Where the hell was my shirt? I went to the closet and grabbed a dress to put on for now. Evan was still lying in my bed when I walked out of my closet and he was stroking his dick.

"Get the fuck out of here now!" I said it in a way that wasn't too loud, but my tone was strong and had definitive meaning. I kept glancing at the door, afraid that Tia would come in and somehow take Evan's side. I asked him where she was.

"Don't worry. She's fast asleep. I made sure of that before coming in here. I was thinking about you the entire time, wishing that it were you I was making love to."

"Ungh-ungh! Get out Evan, before I go wake her up. I'm not playin'." I threatened.

"Do it and she will lose everything I've ever given her. You know whose name this place is in. Whose name do you think is on the title of her car? Who do you think pays all of her bills and buys all of her clothes? Who do you think makes deposits into her bank account? It's not you. It's me. Go ahead, wake her up. I think she'll cut ties with you before losing an extravagant lifestyle she doesn't have to pay for."

I dropped my head. He was probably right about everything he'd said. I don't know. I wasn't in my right state of mind to figure everything out. "What do you want from me, Evan?"

"One night only. You're so fuckin' hot and sexy. I gotta have you."

"No, no, no! I won't do it. I'm not doing Tia like that. You can forget about it."

"$10,000, Nikki. For one night with you. That's it."

$10,000? I never considered it. All money wasn't good money. It was bad enough I'd given him a lap dance and almost got off on it earlier was betrayal enough. "Get out, Evan, please." I turned down his offer. I looked up. He was still fondling that long, big black cock of his. He squeezed the shaft and it seemed to grow bigger. Since he didn't want to leave, I would. I grabbed a suitcase and began packing my things. A lot of bitches in my shoes would have taken the money. In all actuality, $10,000 is a lot of money to have sex with someone for when I'd done it for less before. It wasn't about the money like I said. I was different from most bitches. It was about my belief, morality, and morals, the principles. I respected those who've shown me the utmost respect. Those who'd picked me up when I was down, who'd been nothing but loyal to me. It was my duty to do unto others as they'd done unto me. I loved Tia too much. I just couldn't do it.

Evan had the audacity to proposition me for a role in a movie, plus the money. How naive did he think I was? I told him to go fuck himself and left him chucking that big, beautiful dick. I had to take one last look at it. I could still appreciate a big dick whenever I saw one, couldn't I? Didn't mean I had to suck it or fuck it. After I packed enough for now, I went to Rachel's and told her what had gone down, leaving out the scene at the club. I made her promise to keep it between the two of us. She and Tia were friends, too. I didn't want Rachel slipping up and saying something to her about it. She vowed to never mention it.

"How long is he in town for?" she asked.

"I don't know. All I know is that I don't want to be nowhere near him. I'll be stayin' here until he leaves. That's for sure."

"What will you tell Tia when she asks why you left?"

"I'll just tell her I heard them havin' sex and thought it would be best if I gave them their privacy."

"You do know you're going to hear me, and my boyfriend have sex whenever he's here, don't you? We get loud, especially me."

"You must think I forgot how you get it in?" I laughed.

She and I used to get trains run on us when we were younger. Sometimes, we'd be in the same bed, side by side. Her ass was always loud. Those were the good ol' days. We talked a short while, then we went to sleep.

******

I had a text from Ro when I woke up. He wanted me to call, stating that it was important I did. I waited until I got myself fully together with my every day wake up ritual before I called him.

"Hey. You wanted me to call?" I got straight down to business. To be real, I was slightly upset with him for standing me up last night. He could've called or texted to let me know he wasn't going to show up. He apologized for his inconvenience. His excuse was that something had come up.

"That's not the only reason I wanted you to call. My brother wants to meet you."

"What? When?" I asked excitedly.

"Today. Hell, right now if you're available."

If I wasn't available, I was now. To meet Lil' B is an honor. I told Ro when and he told me the where.

"This meeting can change your life, so be on point, Nikki."

"Say no more." I said and hung up, practically running to my suitcase, hoping like hell I had packed something sexy to wear in it. Favorably, I had. I opted for my black mid-rise skinny jeans and a white top that revealed a lot of cleavage and my navel. The only problem now was that I had left all of my shoes, boots, and heels at Tia's. I didn't have time to drive all the way over there to get them. Luckily for me, Rachel reminded me that I had a few pairs of heels I had left here. One pair was my sheath and ladylike pumps that matched my outfit perfectly. I applied a small amount of makeup then sprayed on my Coco Chanel perfume I'd packed before leaving Tia's and was good to go. I borrowed one of Rachel's necklaces and watches to accentuate my look. I then drove to Buckhead to the Ritz-Carlton to meet Lil' B. Before getting out of my car, there were two things I needed to do. Nose and teeth check. I popped some fresh Double mint gum in my mouth. Nikki Bunz was flawless. Time to make my dream come true.

Chapter Eleven

Ro opened the door to the suite, greeting me with a warm hug.

"You stayin' the night with me and if you're wonderin' am I askin', I'm not." he said. I loved a man who took charge, going after what he wanted.

"I have to work tonight," I replied.

"Say no more. I give you my word I'll be there tonight. You're leavin' with me."

"Is that a question?" I smiled.

"Glad to know we're on the same page."

"Me too. I'm here, so what's up?"

He led me to Lil' B. There were six other people there, including my favorite R&B singer in the world, Josielyn Billups. I was so close to asking her for an autograph. Instead, I kept my cool and spoke to everybody in the room. They all acknowledged me, then Lil' B asked everyone to excuse themselves, so they all left to go into the adjoining room, leaving the two of us alone to talk.

"Have a seat. Want anything to eat? Drink?" Lil' B asked. He was dressed in a cream Burberry shirt and tan Fendi pants and cream Louis Vuitton shoes. I swear he was one of the most beautiful men I had ever seen.

"No, thank you." I sat down, sitting to the left of him, declining his other offers.

"How are you, today?"

"I'm good. How are you?" I asked in return.

"I'm great. Too blessed to be stressed."

"I just bet you are," I laughed. Although I was nervous to be in Lil' B's presence, I still had to be myself. He seemed to like the way I'd said that because he chuckled.

"What do you mean by that?" He was grinning from ear to ear.

"You know exactly what I mean. I know the story of you. Let me correct that, I've read the story about you. There's no rainy day ever in your forecast. I wish I had it like you."

"Mo' money, mo' problems."

"I like to think otherwise. No money, mo' problems."

"That, too. Well anyway, I know you're wonderin' why I wanted to meet with you," I nodded my head. "It's about you being in my movie."

"What about it?" I questioned, hoping he was not about to cut me out of it. He sat straight up, looking at me a little eerie.

"You're a great dancer, don't get me wrong. You did your thang. However, it's not what I want you to do in my movie. I think you'll be perfect for another role. You remind me of somebody."

"Let me guess, Kylie Jenner?"

He laughed. "I wasn't goin' to say her."

"Then who?"

"You remind me of this white girl I once knew. She had a major impact on my life and she's part of the reason why I sit where I am today. When I first saw you, I instantly knew you'd be the perfect one to play her role. You remind me so much of her. Have you ever acted before?"

I was ecstatic, caught up in my emotions, and they began to get the best of me. I felt my eyes water. Damn it, I'm fixing to cry.

"What's wrong? Did I say somethin' to offend you?" Lil' B asked, full of compassion. I shook my head no.

"I-I've never had this kind of opportunity before me. All I've ever been is a stripper," I cried.

I had to force myself not to call myself a whore and a prostitute. He'd probably erase all ideas of turning me into a movie star if he knew my whole past or present. He walked out of the room, leaving me with my tears, but to my utter surprise, he returned with some tissue, and handed it to me.

"You okay?"

"Yea. I'm just happy, that's all. I thought you were about to tell me I had a role as one of the five dancers, but you're offering me somethin' so much better. To answer your question about have I ever acted before, no I haven't. I'm willin' to learn if you're willin' to teach me."

"It's cool if you haven't. We all gotta start somewhere, don't we? I can help get you on point, so don't worry about it. I got somethin' else you may be interested in doin' in the meantime. What do you think about being on a reality TV show?"

"Are you serious?! Really?!" Wait a minute. I was still asleep. This had to be all a dream. Okay, I can wake up now. When I didn't wake up, I knew this was as real as it gets. Lil' B was dead ass serious. He told me he could get me in the reality show called *Love N Da Hood*. The show captured the lives of b-list actors, rappers, singers, and a few unknown people who were from the streets of wherever they were from. It was a hit show and all the episodes were shot here in Atlanta, so that was a definite plus.

"Give me a few weeks to talk to the producers of the show and I'll let you know wassup. Is dat good with you?" Lil' B asked.

"More than you'll ever know."

"Any questions?"

"Why me?" I just had to ask.

"That's a question you have to answer for yourself. Once you answer it, you have to ask yourself what you want out of life. We can always be doin' better with our lives even when we're doin' better. There's always room for improvement."

He asked me something that only my mother, father, and my

teachers had asked. "What do you want out of your life?" When my parents and teachers had asked, I was too young, fast, and rebellious to give a clear and straight answer. While I was in prison, it was something that I put some thought into and came up with what I thought was a master plan. The way Lil' B asked it, it felt like it had more meaning to it, like I needed to rethink my life and come up with a real plan besides stripping and whorin'. Blessings like these didn't come around that much for people like me. I made a promise to myself right then and there. From this day forward, I would put my life into better perspective.

Lil' B and I talked for a good minute. He couldn't believe I'd been to prison before. I told him what I'd done and who I'd done it to, and he cried in laughter.

"That was you?! What did they do to make you do dat?" He was still laughing.

"Let's just say that they fucked over the wrong bitch."

"You do know dat Yasmin used to be on *Love N Da Hood*, don't you?"

"So, I've heard." I said like it was nothing, which it wasn't to be honest.

Lil' B told me he heard that Yasmin had moved back to Memphis and was still doing her thing with her magazine company. I hadn't seen an Urban Heartshapes issue since I've been out. I used to see them all the time while I was locked up. Fuck Yasmin, Alisa, and Cali. Fuck 'em all to hell! I didn't want to talk about them any longer.

Lil' B turned out to be a very chill person. He was humble and had an out of this world sense of humor, which surprised me nonetheless. He was knowledgeable. He was business and street smart and incredibly wise. All in all, he was a Boss! After our talk, he called Ro and the rest of them back in and we all sat around choppin' it up. They sure loved to smoke weed. They fired up blunt after blunt of loud. I was scared I would catch a contact. They made me feel like I was a part of them, especially when they found out I was from Mississippi. We got to trading war stories then. Needless to say, this was by far one of the happiest days of my life. I couldn't wait to call Tia and Shamarah and tell them the good news. I'd tell Rachel when I got back to her place.

I finally told Ro my real name, but not before pulling him out of earshot. I didn't want anyone else to know. It was bad enough Ro did his little he-he and ha-ha, just cracking the fuck up with his ugly, handsome ass.

"I'ma start callin' you Karolina," he laughed.

"And the very first time that you do, I swear it'll be your last time."

"You won't stop fuckin' with me, will you?"

"Yep."

"That's cold-blooded."

We both laughed our asses off. Immediately after we stopped, we had one of those moments like they do in the movies when the man and woman stare at each other all weird before they kiss, then somebody walks in and spoils the moment. That's exactly what happened to us. We were leaning in to kiss when Ro's youngest brother burst in telling Ro that they had to go. One of their nephews had been shot. I was sorry to hear that. Ro apologized and said he would catch up with me later.

"You have nothin' to apologize for. I totally understand. I hope your nephew's alright." I said as we all left. I couldn't help but to think that it wasn't meant for Ro and me to have sex. I sure wanted to. Something seemed to always get in our way. The next time we were together, I was getting some of that dick. I don't care where we were, it was going down right then and there. I put that on my mama. I hoped Ro would be as ready as I would be.

Chapter Twelve

Gucci Mane and the Migos were among a handful of rappers at the club on this lovely Saturday night. They'd grabbed a few of the girls and were enjoying themselves in VIP. I was a bit disappointed that they didn't choose me to come party with them. Guess they didn't like white girls. It didn't matter though. I didn't really feel like dancing tonight anyway or being bothered for that matter. My mind was somewhere else. I was thinking of Ro and Lil' B, wondering if their nephew was alright or not. I hope he wasn't dead.

The more I thought about the conversation Lil' B and I had, the more I wanted to ditch this place. I just wasn't feeling it. I felt like I was about to have an emotional breakdown. I went back to the dressing-room and took a real good look at myself in the mirror. There I stood, silver five-point star stickers covering my nipples and areolas. A silver thong and six-inch stripper heels accentuated my costume. I pulled the platinum blonde wig off my head. This was the only way men knew me. The famous, Nikki Bunz. The one who stripped and fucked for money, whose five-year plan consisted of stripping and fucking my way to even more fame. I also had another plan I wanted to set in motion. It was the plan I'd put together while in prison. I hadn't had the time to start putting things together yet because that time hadn't come to pass yet. I wanted to do amateur porn. I was going to find me a willing partner, whether it be a man or woman and set me up a webcam in my room and charge those interested to watch me work my magic. Later, when I became well known and made a lot of money, I was going to start my own porn company. I thought it was the perfect plan on account of I love having sex for money. Why not build an empire around it? I wasn't good at nothing else. That's what I thought of myself until I had a talk with Lil' B. He made me feel like I could be so much more than a stripper, whore, and prostitute. Amazing how one conversation could bring clarity to a person's life. Lil' B should consider being a preacher or motivational speaker. Those two were key traits to his personality. I looked at myself in the mirror again. I didn't have the guts to look myself eye to eye. I wanted to cry. I wish I had someone to make me feel loved and wanted. My relationship with Money's bitch ass, not only left me physically scarred, but it also left me to the point where I didn't trust men with my emotions or heart. I'd always been told that birds of a feather flock together, that all men are dogs. All but my father. I slammed my fist on the table, fighting the tears on the brink of flooding my eyes.

"Listen up everybody!" I heard the DJ on the mic. "HipHop's royalty just walked in dis bitch! Who? The one and only, Lil' mothafuckin' B!"

What? I thought his nephew had been shot. Guess that meant he was okay. I was immediately upbeat and hurried up and got myself together, putting back on my wig, and running back out on the floor. I saw at least ten bitches flocking to Lil' B and company, hoping to get into VIP with them. I walked up and just as I figured, I was chosen to go in with five other dancers. I don't know where Shamarah came from, but she was amongst the five.

The dudes in Lil' B's circle were him, Ro, their brother Head, four more dudes I didn't know, and six bodyguards. Ro pulled me onto his lap and playfully smacked my butt. "Hey, you gotta pay for that, ya know?" I teased. He pulled out a wad of money similar to the one he'd shown me the first night I met him.

"How much?" he smiled.

"I take it that your nephew is good," I said over one of Lil' B's songs that the DJ was now playing.

"Yea, he good. My sister overreacted about it. He wasn't even hit."

"That's a good thing. Now that your nephew is good, I'm not lettin' you out of my sight." I laughed.

"Is dat right?"

"You'll see."

I was super serious when I said the next time, we were together, I was fucking him. Ain't nothing changed. I needed some dick bad. Hopefully, Ro would fuck me out of my emotional state. I looked over at Lil' B. Shamarah had his full attention. Lil' B must've liked her because he was smiling his ass off. Head had a girl sitting beside him while he broke down a blunt. It wasn't long before the loud filled the atmosphere. The guys ordered six bottles of Ace of Spades. Everybody's cup was filled, including mine. I wasn't a drinker, but I wasn't going to be the party-pooper. We were having ourselves too much of a good time. I drank enough to get a nice little buzz going and inhaled enough weed smoke to get a contact. About an hour later, all of us girls were naked and getting our money.

I was bent over, holding my ankles, making my big white booty wobble. I looked between my legs, placing my hand on my vagina and formed the Peace sign with my fingers. Ro was peering at me with sexual desire. I thought he was going to take me right there in front of everybody while I was locked into this position. I'd taken plenty of dick bent over like this before. I stuck out my tongue, waving it up and down, indicating how I wanted him in my mouth. He was rubbing his hard dick through his designer jeans. I raised up and there was action going on all around me. The room had a long couch that reached wall to wall. Head was dicking down my girl, Pretty Eyez from the back while she sucked on the dick of Lil' B's cousin, Toon. Red and Sneeze were Toon's brothers, and there was Jack, Lil' B's best friend. Ro had told me who everybody was earlier. I looked at Lil' B and Shamarah. They weren't fucking, but if she kept grinding in his lap the way that she was, it wouldn't be long before they were. She looked like she was going to find out the size of his dick after all, and I would be out of a whole hundred dollars when she did. I sat in Ro's lap facing him, throwing my arms around his neck.

"Where can we go, so I can get my private show?" Ro asked. Evidently, he didn't like the group sex/orgy thing. It was all good. A bitch was horny, and I wanted to fuck wherever.

"Let me go check to see if one of the room's available. I'll be right back." I said, putting my thong back on, before grabbing my money. I wasn't leaving without my dough. I didn't pay attention to the other girls and what they were doing because I was too busy trying to get out of there and get back. Before I could open the door, Ro called me back.

"Let's get out of here. Does goin' to my room sound better?" he asked.

"Yea. We can do that. I have to change first. Wait for me at the bar,"

Ro said okay. At that instant, he told Lil' B he was leaving. Lil' B called one of his bodyguards over. While he was telling the dude to leave with Ro, I looked over at Pretty Eyez again. Head was banging her harder now. Toon was trying to insert his dick in her mouth, but she was too occupied, crying out from the pleasure Head was giving her. One of the dancers named Honey Thick walked up and pulled Toon's dick in her mouth.

"Ro, will you please hurry up!" I said, tapping my foot, pussy dripping wet like a leaking faucet. Ro and Lil' B laughed, then Ro and I left so I could go and get dressed. Ensuingly, I walked out of the dressing-room and was startled by Evan wearing another disguise. The man standing behind him must've been his bodyguard. I'm not going to lie, my heartbeat sped up, and Evan was starting to freak me out with his stalker like ways. I tried to walk past him, but he blocked my path.

"What do you want, Evan? Move." I tried to keep my cool.

"You know what I want. My offer still stands as is. Just one night, Nikki,"

"And my answer still stands as is no. Now move!" I tried walking around him again, despite so, he prevented me from doing so.

"Nikki, please. Forget one night. What if I said for a few hours, four tops?" He suggested.

My answer was still a hard, hell to the no. If I did Tia like that and she found out about it, it would most certainly break her heart. Not only that, but she'd also most likely kill me. I wasn't taking a chance on either one. Evan grabbed my butt. For that violation, he received a hard slap to his left jaw. "Don't fuckin' touch me!" I yelled.

"I'ma get what I want. I always do." he exclaimed, looking at me like he wanted to touch me again.

"You'll NEVER EVER get me!"

"Is there a problem here?" I looked in the direction of where Q and his two bodyguards stood. "Nikki, you good?"

"I don't know. Ask Evan am I good or not."

"Evan? You good?"

"Yea, I'm good, Q. I was only having a conversation with the lady."

I didn't know Q and Evan knew each other on a personal level. I told Evan I wasn't interested in any conversation with him now, or one in the future. I began making my way to Ro.

"You're leavin'?" asked Q.

"I have a date." I said, walking past him.

Evan was something else. I had to keep a closer eye on him. He was getting ridiculous with the stunts he was pulling. I thought about telling Tia even though I know it wouldn't do any good. I wasn't going back to her place until Evan was out of town. Better yet, out of the country. I wasn't going to let his shenanigans interfere with my night with Ro. I put all thoughts of Evan on ice. It was time to suck and fuck like the pro I am.

"You ready?" I held out my arm for Ro to take and got the hell out of there.

Chapter Thirteen

At long last, I had Ro exactly where I wanted him. He was sprawled across the bed, dick long and thick, looking like a baby Louisville Slugger covered in latex. I'd been sucking on it the entire ride here. I gotta say, the man has incredible staying power. I had tried every trick in the book to get him to cum for me. Be that as it may, I had another trick up my sleeve. Let's see how long he'll last in this good, hot, tight pussy of mine. I jumped on top of him wanting to ride. I interlocked my fingers with his, planting my feet flat on the bed, and squatted down slowly on him. Oh God, I could feel him in my stomach. I clasped my vaginal muscles tight, grinding on him moderately. I moved my hips in a circular motion, imitating the hands on the clock. Oh yes! I grinded harder, pussy still gripping him, as I moved counterclockwise. Oh hell, yes! The pleasure of my technique caused him to grunt, to say my name. I began rocking back and forth. Faster. Harder. I slowed down a little. Slower. Faster, again. I bounced up and down, fucking him like he had never been fucked before. He called out my name again. I rose up until only the tip of his dick was inside of me, my pussy grabbing his dickhead in a bear hug as I moved my hips from left to right. I carried on like this until I loosened my hold on him and slammed down to continue my ride on his love stick.

"Ssss...Ssssss..." He was loving every second of it. I was riding him so fast our bodies slapped hard against each other. "F-f-fu--fu-fuck, Nikki!"

"You like the way my pussy fuckin' you?" I asked, breathing hard, running out of breath.

"Hell yea! Do dat shit!"

I resumed my quest to get him to cum for me. Instead, I was the one who was on the verge of a powerful orgasm. I knew it wouldn't be much longer because his dick is the truth. Using my muscles, I navigated it to the spot that always makes me cum whenever I'm on top. Seconds later, voila.

"Ooooouuuu, Rooo! I'm cummin', boyyy! I'm cummin' for youuuu! Oooouuu-ssshhhiiitttt!" That shit felt astoundingly good. I was shaking on top of him. I released my hands in addition to squeezing my breasts. Ro rose up from the bed, going back and forth sucking on my nipples. "Bite it," I commanded, holding a titty out for him. "Ssss-mmmmm! Harder! Ohhhh!" The pain sent waves of pleasure racing to my throbbing clit. I pulled my abandoned breast to my mouth, flicking my tongue across my nipple. Then, as Ro bit a nipple, matching his intensity, so did I.

A good five seconds passed, and I was cumming again. As soon as I finished, I fell backwards, head hanging at the foot of the bed, catching my breath. I felt Ro get out of bed. Moments later, I heard him striking a lighter, firing up yet another blunt. He had been smoking in my car throughout the time I was giving him head. At the thought of that, "Come put it in my mouth," I said as I rammed two fingers into my glistening cunt.

Ro positioned himself over my head, removing the Magnum. He grabbed his dick at the base and slapped my face a few times before sitting his balls on my lips. In a New York minute, I went to work on them, sucking one, then both, humming my favorite tune as I did.

"Damnnn! So freaky and nasty!" he groaned.

"Mmm-hmmm." I mumbled, continuing my buzzing effect on his nuts. After a while, I pushed him backwards in readiness to have him in my mouth. I grabbed his long, fat cock and pulled him in.

"Move your hand," he said. I conformed to his demand, letting him fuck my mouth slowly while he smoked his blunt.

He reached over me, proceeding to finger-fuck me fast with two fingers. Next thing I knew, he pulled away then placed his fingers in my mouth.

"Mmmmmmmmmm...mmngh!" I gobbled up my juices. He put his dick back in my mouth, pushing it in deep until I gagged, and tapped his thigh for him to stop right there. My throat couldn't fit another inch in it. Ro took a whole step back. Guess he'd had enough of getting his dick sucked. He sat the blunt in the ashtray before putting on a fresh condom.

"How do you want it, baby?" I was laid on my back, slapping my pussy gently. He turned me around. Lifting my legs, he pushed them all the way to the back until my ass rose from the bed. He pushed me backwards as he climbed into bed with me. He was in the push-up position about to work out on me. The best thing about it, I couldn't move. I was at his complete mercy. He dropped that big ass dick in me and went to work on my little ass.

"Oooh, fuck me! Ooouuu, Ro dick me down just like that, baby! Ohh dammmnnnn, Ro! Mmngh-ungh... Mmmmmm!" He beat my pussy rhythmically. "Oooouuuu, you beatin' this pussy up! It hurts so good, Roooo! It hurts sooooo good!" All I could do was make my pussy clamp down as he continued laying that black pipe in me.

"Pussy so fuckin' tight! Unnghhh!" He growled, obviously loving the way my pussy was feeling to him. I knew how to make a man scream. I got some good pussy and I knew how to use it. Men always loved when my pussy fastened around their cocks.

"You like it, Ro? Get it then. Beat this pussy like you mad at me! That's it! C'mon, don't be scared! Fuck me hard baby!" My body burst into convulsion as I came again. Meanwhile, Ro snarled in an animal-like sound, filling the Magnum with his sperm. Oh, how I wished he'd come in my mouth instead.

He released my legs, easing into the regular missionary position as we caught our breaths. He stayed inside of me until his engorged cock fell limp. He rolled off of me, asking me did I want to take a shower.

Under the warm water, we took turns washing each other's privates. I resisted the urge to suck his dick some more. He took the gumption to bend me over and he ate my pussy and ass like they were an icy white honey bun. Undoubtedly, I came again. I'd lost count of how many times Ro made me cum. He went to sleep holding me, but the next morning, I awoke, and he was gone. He'd left me $2,000 along with a note saying that he had to leave with Lil' B on a business trip out of town and he didn't want to awake me. He said the room and the suite was paid for the next three days and I was welcomed to stay if I wanted to. Hell yes, I was going to stay. Why the hell wouldn't I? This was the peace and quiet I needed to think some things through. One thing in particular, I needed to start looking for my own place. I didn't want to take the chance of being around Evan ever again. Especially after the stunt he'd pulled on me last night. Somehow, I knew we'd have to come face to face again.

Chapter Fourteen

I was going live on Instagram, flirting with and teasing my fans and followers. I was prancing around the suite in a wife beater and a pair of pink boy shorts. Every so often, I would drop low and twerk for them. Some of the men left messages on my live feed, complimenting me on how pretty and fine I am. Some of them left messages wanting to spend some money on me for a private show or wanted me to perform for them on their birthdays or whatever. Some of their offers were just plain ridiculous, thinking that I was going to be their woman. I was reading their messages when I saw that Tia had sent one telling me to check my DM. I paused my live feed to see what my girl wanted. She was curious about where I was because she wanted to talk. I got off IG and called her.

"What's up, bitch? What's goin' on?" I asked.

"Checkin' in to see where you were. From the looks of it, looks like you're doin' big things. Tell me where you are, I wanna come through. We haven't really kicked it since you've been home."

"I know right." She had a point. We hadn't had our normal talks, girl's not out, or nothing. I've been working my ass off, if I can call it that, and she's been busy chilling with Evan. Man, I hated to think of that dude. I told her where I was and when she arrived, we ordered food and champagne and sat back and relaxed until our orders arrived.

She wanted to know everything I knew about Lil' B. I didn't have much to tell her about him, nothing but what my personal opinions were of him. She asked me about Ro and had I fucked him yet.

"One of the few times I've been fucked to sleep," I bragged on Ro's amazing sex game.

"Everything seems to be workin' in your favor. I'm so proud of you and I'm happy for you, Nikki. My girl's about to be a movie star and reality star. You're gonna kill it. I believe in you 1,000%," She hugged me.

"I hope I don't somehow mess this up."

"Ungh-ungh. Don't you dare talk that up. You do know that you can speak things into existence? Nope. From now on, you're only speakin' positive things to happen in your life," she advised me, shutting down all my naysaying. Tia was my rock. She always kept me balanced in my life. Honestly, I didn't know where I'd be without her. Nevertheless, I could sense that something was bothering her. She had something to say, but was struggling with how to tell me.

"What's wrong? Everything's 10-10?" Before she could answer me, room service arrived. We got a few bites into our fish and sipped some of the champagne in our chutes before I asked her again.

"It's Evan. For some apparent reason, he doesn't trust you and don't want you livin' with me anymore."

"Huh?! What?! He said that?!" I couldn't believe Evan had the dauntlessness to say that bullshit when he's the motherfucker that can't be trusted. I should tell on his ass right now, but I waited to see how this would finish playing out first.

"Yes, he said it," Tia said, not able to look me in my eyes. "That's not all. He brought up about you being an ex-convict and claims that the other night while he was using the bathroom, you walked in naked tryin' to get him to have sex with you."

"What?! He's lyin'. I swear on my mama he is!"

"I know you wouldn't do me like that. All this time you've known me, you've never known me to be nobody's fool. I noticed that you've taken majority of your things from my place. I think the reason you did that was probably somethin' Evan had done to you and you being you, you didn't want to tell me. To be honest, I don't want to know what he did. When I told him, I didn't believe what he was claimin' you did, he slapped me around a few times, threatening to take everything from me if I ever took your side again. He wants me to kick you out or he's goin' to do it. I'm sorry, Nikki. You know I'm in no position to lose everything. I have to think about my boys." She broke into a sob, crying on my shoulders.

I could respect that. As a friend, I wouldn't want to put her under that kind of pressure when I had a place, I could lay my head every night, still. It was pointless to tell her the things Evan had done. By him laying hands on her, she'd already declared that he could do whatever and she would forgive him. The things people resign themselves to. I couldn't judge her. I've made sacrifices myself. I wasn't mad with her nor was I going to look at her any different. She would always be my friend, and when friends need each other, we step the fuck up and be there for them. I let her cry her sorrows away, all the while, I was telling her that everything between us was good and would remain that way. I asked her how long Evan was in town for because I needed to get the rest of my things from her place. His ass was in town for business for the next few weeks. After Tia's tears, we ordered some more room service. I'd already talked to Ro about the bill. He gave me a number not to exceed. If I did, it would go on my tab.

Any who, I called Rachel and Shamarah to invite them to the suite. Might as well turn this into a girl's day filled with massages, mani's, pedi's, great food, and champagne. Rachel arrived first. Shamarah came through the door fifteen minutes later wanting her hundred dollars off bat, as she bragged about her having already stayed a night here. She revealed pieces of her and Lil' B's night together.

"So, is his dick as big as you imagined it would be?" I had to ask since she made me pay my debt.

"Bitch, yasss! His lil' ass knows how to slang it too! I can't count the number of times I came."

"Shoot! His brother had me the same exact way. I'm still tryin' to remember how many times I nutted. I lost count somewhere around five, I think," I boasted. I had to throw my night in too, so Shamarah wouldn't think she was the only one having back to back, mind-blowing orgasms.

"I'm so jealous."

"Me, too," Rachel and Tia chimed in. "Sounds like I need to get back on the scene," Tia joked. For some reason, I thought about Evan and his hoe-like ways he'd been on recently. I had to find a way to get him back without hurting Tia in the process. Fuck Evan! He wasn't worth my time. I continued enjoying my day with the people I loved and who loved me.

******

"Good afternoon, Ms. Musgraves. Have a seat," My probation officer said.

She had called me in today. For what, I had the slightest clue. I had been out of prison now going on three weeks and my monthly scheduled appointment wasn't for another two weeks. I was kinda nervous to say the least. It was never good when they wanted you to come in early. I took a seat, waiting to see what this was all about.

"I'll get right down to why I called you in, so you can get on with your day, I hope."

She hoped? What the hell did that supposed to mean? Didn't sound good at all.

"It's been brought to my attention that you're a stripper."

"Yes ma'am, I am," I replied with no shame at all. "May I ask what that has to do with my visit today?"

"See the thing is, you're not allowed to be in that kind of setting. I know what goes on in places like that. There's a lot of drugs in those places. Not to mention, guns, ex-convicts, which all equals violence. You're not allowed to be in a strip club nor working in one."

She sure knew an awful lot about strip clubs. Made me wonder how she knew so much about them. To come to think about it, she has a body like a stripper. Maybe, she used to be one before starting her career in criminal justice. The main thing that had me puzzled was the mere fact that she knew I danced for a living. How did she know? Had she seen me herself? Did somebody tell her? If the latter, then who? I couldn't come up with a single suspect.

"I'm sorry Ms. Musgraves, but you're going to have to quit your job. There's plenty of other jobs you can con-"

Her words drowned out. I couldn't believe this shit! Stupid bitch telling me I have to quit the one thing I loved doing. She better be glad Lil' B had something else for me to do with my life. If not for that, I'd go work at another club. Preferably, Magic City. Speaking of Lil' B, I still hadn't heard back from him on getting me on the reality show. I'd talked to Ro numerous times in the span of two weeks. All he said was to give it some time. "What's meant for you is meant for you," He calmed my anxieties. I was still looking at Ms. Taylor move her lips, so I started back listening to her. She's saying something very important now.

"If I hear about you still working at that club, you're going to be in direct violation of your probation, and I'll send you back to prison. Do I make myself clear?"

"Crystal," I said with a hint of sarcasm. "Can I at least go and get all of my belongings I have there in my locker? I have some important things in my locker."

Her eyes scrutinized me as she mulled over my request. "In and out, Ms. Musgraves. I'm not playing with you." She said, wagging her finger at me like I was her child.

"In and out. I swear. Will that be all?"

"One more thing before you go," She went inside her desk and produced a drug test. I had to piss in the cup, damn! I passed with flying colors and left her office en route to the Blue Flame.

Ever had the feeling you were being watched? I had this uncanny feeling that I was. Maybe I was just paranoid, overreacting from what Ms. Taylor had said. I felt like she had somebody watching me. Fine. I admit it, I was trippin'. I made it to the club and got all of my things out of my locker. I went to Q's office to tell him the news. His ass had two bitches in there sucking his dick, and they kept sucking like I wasn't even there. Q peered at me like he was about to cum in any second, asking me what I wanted. When I told him about my visit to my P.O.'s office and that she wanted me to quit working here, he dismissed the girls, and fixed his clothes so we could talk. He didn't like it and wanted to know if there was anything he could do to help keep me on. I told him there was nothing he could do to fix this.

"Fuck it. It is what it is." I said, then talked to him about Lil' B.

"I've done time with Lil' B before. A long time ago when we were in Boot Camp. He's one hunnid. If he says he's goin' to help you, that's what he's goin' to do. He keeps his word every time he gives it. I'm happy for you, Nikki. You're one of dem people who deserves the opportunities in your hands. Do yo' thang, you hear? Don't let anyone stand in the way of you tryin' to block your shine. If you ever need me, you got my number. Don't hesitate to hit me up."

"I won't," I said, shocked that he and Lil' B had done time together when they were teenagers. I always knew that Q was originally from Tupelo, Mississippi. That was the main reason we got along so good.

"I got an idea."

"Oh, shit! Q's got an idea," I laughed.

"Ha-ha, whatever, nigga. Anyway, what you think about havin' a retirement party here?"

"I don't know, Q. Did you just hear one word I said about my P.O.?" Didn't I just tell this fool I could go back to prison if I got caught being here.

"That's easy to fix," he said.

"How so?"

"I'll shut the club down and we'll just invite the girls that work here and some of your trusted clients. Nobody else. What you think?"

Since he put it that way, I thought it was an excellent idea. Nikki Bunz would go out in fashion as a former stripper. I'm not going to lie, I was sad that I had to quit. I mean, I love this place and I would always be connected to it in some form. I had made so much money inside the Blue Flame. I was definitely going to miss the life. "When were you talkin' about throwin' the party?" I asked.

"I'm thinkin' next Tuesday would be perfect."

"Club goin' up, on a Tuesday! Hell yea, let's do it!" I exclaimed, loving the idea.

We planned some more on the party. Q said he had some surprised guests he would have there for me. I asked who, but he wouldn't tell me. He knew a lot of celebs and all kinds of characters. I was roused up on who he would get to come on such short notice. However, I was excited about my retirement party. I went home. I was living with Rachel now. I told her about my day, then called Tia and Shamarah on a conference call to tell them. They said they were sorry to hear that I'd been forced to quit. I asked Tia if she was coming to my party. She said no because she and Evan were going somewhere private to have a good time. Shamarah said she would most certainly be there.

When Tuesday night came, we had the club looking like a Friday or Saturday in that bitch. It was super lit.

Q's surprise for me was one I would never forget. He had gotten three of my favorite porn stars to show up for my party. Go-Go Fuk Me, Chanelle Heart, and Kelly Devine were in the building. The bigger surprise was when they called me on stage to sit in a chair so they could give me a lap dance and strip for me. I sat there entertained as they put their titties, pussy, and ass all in my face. I had so much fun with them. After that, I gave my last and final performance as a stripper. I danced better than I had ever danced before. I was turnt all the way up. Shamarah and Rachel had talked me into drinking a little liquor. I wasn't drunk, just buzzing. That was by far the most fun I had in a very long time.

When the night was over, I was driving Rachel and I home. I messed around and swerved a little, almost running head on with a car. I don't know how I managed to do that. Blue lights lit up in my rearview.

"Gotdamn it, Nikki!" I screamed, startling Rachel who was semi-asleep.

"What's goin' on? What did you do?" she asked as I pulled my car over.

"I swerved. Damn it, I didn't know the police were behind us."

"Pop some gum in your mouth," Rachel suggested.

"I don't have any. Do you?" She shook her head as I watched the officer get out of his car. Not me. Not now. I was fucked. There goes that tap on my window that was about to determine my future. I knew I shouldn't have let Q talk me into having that damn party.

"Roll your down your window." I reluctantly did as I was told. "License and registration, please." He was a fairly handsome white man. He looked no older than thirty. I already had my license and registration ready for him. I didn't ask him why he'd pulled me over. That would be an insult if I did. I handed him my paperwork. He studied it, then me.

"You know why I pulled you over?"

"Yes, sir. I was trying to dodge somethin' in the road. I'm sorry."

"Have you been drinkin'?"

"No, sir."

"Step out of the car, ma'am."

"May I ask why?" I was scared now. He repeated himself. This time, I followed orders. He looked me up and down as I stood there with my arms folded.

"Why'd you lie to me about you haven't been drinkin'? I can clearly smell it on your breath. That's the reason I asked. Now again, have you been drinkin'?"

I nodded my head, apologizing, for lying to him. I was looking as sad as I could. He asked me how many drinks I had consumed. I told him only two, which I was still lying about. He looked me up and down again. Next thing I knew, I had to take a breathalyzer and field sobriety tests.

"I'm sorry ma'am, but I have to take you to jail."

"What?! Sir, please no! Please, I just got out of prison a few weeks ago. I was at a party with my cousin and didn't want to be there to begin with. They talked me into havin' a few drinks. I'm not even a drinker like that. Please, don't take me to jail."

"I'm sorry. I gave you an opportunity to tell me the truth and you chose not to." He said, reaching for his handcuffs. "Place your hands behind your back,"

"Please don't take me to jail! I'm sorry! I swear I am! My P.O. is goin' to send me back to prison! I don't want to go back! I hate it there! Sir, please! Is there anything I can do for you to let me off with a warnin'? Just name and I'll do it! I don't wanna go back to prison!" I cried. I pleaded. I begged him not to take me to jail. I was dead ass serious when I said I'd do anything to avoid going to jail.

Turns out, there was something he wanted in exchange for not taking me to jail. Yep, I took him to Rachel's. I had to. He wanted his dick sucked if wanted my get out of jail free card. That was not even the worse part. Rachel had to suck his dick, too. That was the agreement. She and I had to give him some head at the same time. Although Rachel was furious, she didn't want me to go back to prison knowing that she could've done something to prevent it. Her only demand to Mr. Crooked Officer was that she and I weren't touching each other in any kind of way, so he may as well not even conjure up any thoughts of us two. However, while we were sucking his cock, our lips couldn't help but touch. He had a nice sized cock. I was on one side of the officer's dick and she was sucking on the other side. Imagine us both trying to suck the head at the same time. Whenever that happened, one of us would suck on his nuts or just lick down the side of his shaft. We'd still manage to touch lips though. It was hard not to. I didn't care. Cousin or not, Mr. Officer could've told me to eat Rachel's pussy and I would have with no hesitation if it meant that I wasn't going back to prison.

That night was definitely a hard lesson learned for me. No more drinking and trying to drive. No indeed. The following morning, I went to the bank to withdraw $2,500 to give to Rachel for what she'd done for me. I couldn't thank her enough for her contribution. I know some of y'all are casting judgement on me as I speak. I know y'all think I'm crazy if I would eat my own cousin's pussy just to stay out of prison. So, what if I'm crazy in your eyes. But none of you has had to go through the things I had to go through in prison so it's easy for you to judge me. Can I ask you to hold your judgements until you hear the reason why I would sacrifice in that fashion if I had to? I would make any sacrifice if needed to stay out of prison. Here was my reason why.

Zion

Chapter Fifteen

My first six months in, I can't count how many times I was raped by my fat, black, stinky, dyke cellmate, and her seven-bitch clique. As soon as I stepped foot in that prison, I was bullied, raped, robbed, extorted, and used and abused physically, mentally, and emotionally. Later, I learned that it was something almost every newcomer had to endure. The only way you wouldn't have to is, you were a gang member, or well known in the streets or prison, or somebody knew someone in your family. To minimize some of the hardships, you either had to join one of the gangs, become a girlfriend, wife, or side piece to one of them lesbian bitches. Me, I was just a regular Joe. Indeed, I was square and didn't know nothing about doing time in prison. I was just an ex-stripper and urban model with no street ties whatsoever, so I had no knowledge of the gangs these girls were affiliated with. I didn't even deal with street dudes or gang members. I had tried twice, I know for a fact, and both times I did, I was put into some unbelievable situations.

One time, I had been with this guy who had a beef with somebody where I had to end up ducking bullets while their dumb asses shot back and forth at each other. The guy I was with had been shot twice, but he managed to survive. The other time I called myself messing with a street dude, I got jumped on by his baby's mother and three of the girl's family members. That was it for me forever fucking with a dude who ran the streets. Too much drama was attached with them. I swore I would never fuck with one again. It wasn't my thing.

I didn't have any interest in joining any of the girl's cliques or gangs. I wasn't engrossed in becoming nobody's bitch, wife, or whatever. I wasn't there for all of that. I was only there to do my time, get it over with, so I could go home.

When I saw my cellmate, I knew my time wouldn't be easy. Her first words when she saw me was, "Damn! Fine ass white girl." She was extra friendly, helping me with my things and making up my bed. She introduced herself as Roxanne, telling me how much time she'd done and how much she had left. I told her my name then she asked me questions about where I was from, how old I was, what I'd done to get here, because she thought I didn't look the type to be in prison. She told me how things went down on the tier, who was who, and who I shouldn't involve myself with. She asked me had I ever been intimate with a woman before. Of course, I lied like I hadn't. I could tell she was attracted to me in a major way. That lustful ass look she had given her away. I guess she thought bragging on herself would make me want to be with her. She wouldn't stop talking about who she was and how she ran things around here. Supposedly, she was the head bitch in charge on the tier. She had a lot of commissary, explaining to me that she ran a store. I asked her what that meant, and she explained to me the two for one policy. Two for one meant that if I got one item from her, I would have to give her two of the same items back. Seemed like a good hustle to me.

A little later, three of her friends came in. One was a black girl, the other two were Mexican. Neither of them was fat nor ugly like my cellmate. They were cute. I wondered if they had wives or girlfriends. Roxanne was telling them about me and me about them. We all chilled in the cell for a good minute until it was feeding time. I had no choice but to go to the dining hall with them since they were practically the only people I knew at the time. I was thinking that it wasn't so bad and let my guard down. Hell, I do that for? Big mistake. Later that night when it was time for the lights to go out, Roxanne closed the door and made her move on me.

She was saying all kinds of shit like, how she could protect me if I let her. She showed me at dinner all the other gangs and cliques and who their leaders were, trying to scare me into thinking that if I didn't roll with her and her clique, the other girls would make me a victim of their abuse. In the next breath, Roxanne was telling me how fine, sexy, and beautiful I was, how she loved the color of my hair and eyes. She tried every trick in the book to get me to sleep with her. If she were prettier, then maybe I would've considered it. The truth is, looking in Roxanne's ugly fat face was a complete turn off. I kept refusing her advances until she finally pulled out a shank and put it to my throat.

"You can either give it to me or I'ma take it and then cut your fuckin' throat, white bitch."

I was frightened, almost pissing myself. Nobody told me this part of the game. I should have talked to more people about the things that go on in a women's prison. I should've researched Google and YouTube to get up on game when I had the chance. I was in over my head. Tears streamed down my face as the tip of her shank pierced my skin.

"Okay! Okay!" I said a little loud, slick trying to sound the alarm to the guards.

"Shut the fuck up with all that hollerin'! No one's comin' to save you. The police don't give a fuck about you. You should've done this the easy way, hoe. Got me actin' all crazy and shit." Roxanne was more upset than I was. How that was even possible, I don't know.

She pushed me on her bed and began stripping me of my clothes.

"Oh, shit! Look at this pretty pink pussy with red hair and all. Mmm-mmngh! I'm finna have fun with you. Real talk!" She forced my legs open and dove in, all the while, I lay there numb, crying to God asking Him why me? Why did I have to be sent to this place? Why? I know what I did to get here was wrong, but wasn't there a better prison somewhere in Georgia he could've sent me? Was this how they all operated? After she was done eating me out, I thought she was finished. I was getting up when she said, "Where you think you goin'? I'm not done with you. Get on your knees."

"Roxanne, please. That should be enough." *Smack! Smack! Smack!* This bitch slapped me three hard times making me see stars. I sobbed even more.

"I'm not gon' tell you again to get on your knees. Turn dat ass around, now!" I did as she said even though it felt like I had a concussion. I waited to feel her nasty ass tongue on me again. Instead, she inserted a make-shift dildo inside of me and began violating me over and over again for hours on hand. She wanted me to moan because I wouldn't at first. I had no choice to fake like I was enjoying what she was doing, or she was going to beat my ass some more. I definitely wasn't going to risk her stabbing me.

That night would turn into many more. There were times when I would fight back, but it did me no good. She always overpowered me, making me submit when I grew tired of her punching on me. That shit hurt. Sometimes it would happen in the daytime. Sometimes in the showers. I remember one day she made me eat her and her whole clique in the cell. Other times females would pay Roxanne to have their way with me. I felt so ashamed, so embarrassed by what was happening to me and I couldn't do nothing to stop it. No one offered to help me, not even the guards when I wrote them notes, telling them what was occurring under their watch and care. Roxanne was right, the guards didn't care. As I endured the pain I was going through, I still refused to be Roxanne's pet, wife, girlfriend, or bitch. I'd imagined killing Roxanne in a thousand ways. I wasn't going to let her break me. I wasn't going to let her see me cry another tear. I'd cried so many tears that I had none left to cry. I was going to show Roxanne that I had control, not her. I came up with a plan. I was getting off this tier.

One day the guards came around to count. It would always be two of them and they would make us stand outside of our cells while they counted. As soon as they counted me, I punched the one closest to me and went to work on her. I wasn't trying to really hurt her. I just did what I had to. It wasn't long before I was getting jumped on by the other one, then both of them. Before I knew it, there were more guards coming to join in. They beat my ass good and I appreciated it more than they'd ever know. I was thrown in the hole and was beat up some more. The warden had come to talk to me days later, which I refused to open my mouth. I had sent her too many letters about my situation. She didn't care about me, either. She told me she was considering charging me with assaulting her officers. At that point, I didn't give two fucks what they charged me with. I'd already given up in my spirit. I wanted out of that tier. That's all that mattered to me. No one knew how close I came to killing myself. I was fed up with life. About a week later, the guard who I'd punched came to talk to me. She told me she'd done some investigating on me, asking a few inmates the reason I'd pulled that kind of stunt. She said she understood and wasn't going to press any charges on me.

"On one condition," she said.

"What's that?" I asked, my first words in a week.

"You have to apologize."

My chin hit my chest and I cried and cried. "I'm sorry. I wasn't tryin' to hurt you. I just needed to get away from that environment. I couldn't take no more of it. I'd had enough." I looked at her and saw water in her eyes. She felt compassion for me.

"I feel you. Sometimes we just gotta do what we gotta do to stand up for what we believe in. If I were in your shoes, I would have done the same thing."

"I'm sorry, Officer?"

"Hill. Officer Hill,"

"Thank you, Officer Hill. You don't know how much this means to me."

She smiled and walked away, and I would never see her again. A week later, the warden had me transferred to another prison. It was nothing compared to the one I'd escaped from as far as the rapes and all the other bullshit, but I did get into a couple of catfights. One time I was cut by this girl because she refused to pay me back on a two for one. I'd started a store after seeing that no one else ran one. I'd loaned her some deodorant and she was supposed to pay me back on the day our commissary orders came. When it did, she didn't make store and instead of coming to talk to me about it, she chose to avoid me. I gave her ample time to have a conversation with me. Finally, I went to her and asked her where my stuff was, and the bitch beat me getting mad. How dare she. We got into a fight where she pulled out a shank and stabbed me in the arm. I went to the infirmary, having to go off-site to a hospital to get six stitches. After that fight, I had to get a shank of my own. I paid one of the girls who worked in the kitchen to make me one. Prison taught me to never go back. That was the lesson I learned from my time there.

So, now I've given y'all the rundown, can you feel me now? There was no way I was going back to that torcher dome of a place. No fuckin' way! I'll do anything to never go back and I stand on it to my dying day. Love me or hate me, I don't care.

Chapter Sixteen

I found an apartment not that far from Tia's, in a complex right beside Martin Luther King Jr. Park called Castleberry Apartments. Shamarah had helped me in getting the place. She had an aunt who lived there. Thank God she did. The process was much easier than I expected it to be. Two and a half weeks wasn't so bad. My apartment had two bedrooms. It was small, but to my liking. It was perfect for me. The rent's doable. All I needed was a steady job, one that would get me P.O. the hell off my back. She'd been riding me about finding a job like it was easy to find one or something. If my money got to looking funny, I still had a few clients I could call to make my bread look serious again.

As of now, I didn't have much furniture. This was only my fourth day being here. I had a 50" flatscreen TV and a loveseat in the living room, a table with only two chairs in the kitchen. The spare bedroom was pretty much empty, and my room had a queen-sized bed Tia had given me and a 32" flatscreen. In due time, I was going to make my place a home. Shamarah was here with me on this Thursday afternoon. We were coolin' it in my bedroom lyin' in bed naked. The TV was on, but neither of us was watching it. I was working on a Sudoku puzzle while Shamarah massaged my feet. Every so often, she would suck on my big toe.

"I love it when you paint your toenails red. It makes your toes so much prettier," she said, biting my toe playfully.

"Is that the only time my toes are pretty to you?" I teased.

"No. But it's the only time my freaky ass wants to suck on them," We laughed as I returned to my puzzle.

I loved working Sudoku puzzles. They were good exercise for the brain. I had learned to work them when I was in prison and have been addicted to them ever since. I used to have my parents, Tia, Rachel, and Shamarah order them for me all the time. Whenever I had the peace and quiet to work one, I was locked in on them.

"Babe, will you please put down the damn puzzle and come sit on my face?" Shamarah asked me with that look in her eyes that I've never been able to resist. She was so pretty. I loved looking in her face trying to count all of her freckles in her face. I had never been able to count them all because she had so many of them. Shamarah kept it real with me as much as she could when I was locked up. She never came to visit, nor did she write me any letters. She did put money on my commissary and on the phone so we could talk. She was my baby. I would always love her, forever and a day, no matter what.

She was kissing up my leg, making her way to my calf. I parted my legs for her, knowing the location of her destination. I sat the Sudoku puzzle book down when I felt her tongue on my thigh. She kissed me there, suckling my skin, leaving a passion mark. She marked me then made her way further up. I watched her peel back the hood of my clitoris and blow her cool breath on it.

"Sssss-mmngh!" I moaned deeply in pleasure as she administered her next move. She held out the tip of her tongue, flicking it up and down. "Sha-Shamarah! Ohh, babe!" I cried out.

"Mmmmhmmmm..." she mumbled on my clit, feasting away. Just as my hands grabbed my breasts, my phone began playing Lil' B's song, *So Helluva-Live*.

Oh my God, he'd finally called. It took him long enough. I told Shamarah who was calling and told her to stop, but she kept eating me sumptuously. I even tried pushing her head back. Still, she wanted my pussy covered by her talented mouth. Fuck it, let her stay, I thought. I wasn't missing Lil' B's call.

"Hel-hello," I mustered up all the strength I could.

"Can I speak with Karolina with a K?" Lil' B laughed, knowing damn well I told him I didn't like my name. I knew I shouldn't have told him.

"Somebody got jokes today. I don't know. Can you speak with her?" I asked, laughing along with him.

"May I speak with Karolina with a K?"

"Yes, you m-may. What's good, Mr. Brodrick?" I had to bite my hand to keep from moaning. Shamarah sucked on my clit harder after hearing Lil' B's name. She knew what she was doing with her messy ass.

"I was callin' you with good news."

"Oh, yeaaa? Ahhh!" I couldn't help myself. I tried not to whimper, but Shamarah had swirled her tongue around my clit like it was an ice cream cone, sucking it gently. She wanted Lil' B to hear me.

"Did I catch you at a bad time? It sounds like you're havin' sex. Are you?" Lil' B was curious. I could tell he wanted me to say yes. I wanted to say no, however, I wondered what he would say if I told him the truth. damn it, here goes nothing.

"I'm gettin' my pussy ate."

"Oh, o-kay," he stuttered. "I'll let you and yo' boy finish up. Call me as soon as you're done."

I should've said okay. Needless to say, I told him who was eating my pussy. He didn't want to hang up now. In fact, he asked.

"Is she makin' you feel good?" I was a bit surprised by Lil' B's boldness, nevertheless, I was turned on by it.

"Yasss! She's makin' me feel good. Mmmmm. Mmmngh!"

"Tell me how good it feels."

121

"It feels soooo good, B."

"Now tell Shamarah."

I looked at Shamarah. "Babe, it feels incredible." Then closed my eyes, visualizing Lil' B sucking on my clitoris the way Shamarah was.

"You wish you were makin' me feel this good, B?" I provoked him to engage further in our conversation. There was no turning back now. I asked him where he was because I wanted him to pull his dick out and beat it for me. Unfortunately, he was around someone, but he'd walked away to entertain me.

"Is that dick hard? Shamarah says it's so big. I wish I could suck it. I bet it tastes divine. You gon' let me suck your dick and taste your cum the way you let Shamarah?"

"Is dat what you want?"

"Yes, daddy. That's what I want. That's what I need! Oooouuu fuck, Shamarah! Like that, baby! Lil' B wants you to eat my pussy like that! Mmmm!" I was so turned on, pussy extremely wet.

"Think you can suck my dick better than Shamarah?" Lil' B breathed hard into the phone.

"Absolutely."

"How would you suck it if I let you?"

I told him I would spit all over it because I loved to give sloppy toppy. Then, I would suck as much of him as my throat would allow, that my goal would be to deepthroat every fuckin' inch of him. I told him to visualize his entire dick in my mouth, me shaking my head from left to right like a dog when its owner got a towel in its mouth.

"Fuck my mouth like it's a pussy. It turns me on when I'm gaggin' and chokin' on a big dick. I love grabbin' a dick at the base, takin' it to beat my face with it. Would you like to beat my face with your hard cock, B? Oooooouuuuu, fu-

fuuccccckkkkk! B, I wish you were fuckin' me right now. Tell me how you would punish my tight pussy if you were up in it right now."

He said he would make me take him from the back, telling me how hard he'd pull my hair throughout the time he'd be fuckin' me. He admitted that ever since he'd seen me, he'd been thinking about fuckin' me like I was his little slut. He confessed to having had dreams about me, fantasies of fuckin' me in the ass and all. My pussy gushed, listening to him talk dirty to me, especially when he called me his little slut.

"I would love for you to fuck me in my ass. It's so tight," I moaned louder. "I'll be throwing it back, lookin' at you while meetin' your hard thrusts. You know what I would be tellin' you, B?"

"What?"

"Fuck my ass harder, baby! Don't play with it. Give it to me! Fuck my assss!" I think Shamarah took that as her que to lick my ass because I felt her tongue swiping at it. "Give it to me! All that dick in my ass, B! Is that what you want? To fuck my ass hard. Pound it out?" Shamarah's tongue was licking my ass faster.

"Your ass. Your pussy. Your mouth. I want all of you, Nikki," Lil' B must've found some privacy to beat his meat. It sure sounded like he was about to nut.

"I want you to have every hole that your dick can fit in. Do as you please. I'm your little slut, remember? All I wanna be is your nasty bitch. Ooouuuu! Oooouuuuuu! Sha-Shamarah. Da-da-dammnnn!" She had so much of her tongue inside my ass, head bobbing up and down, I thought I was going to faint from the pleasure.

"You sound like you're about to cum in her mouth."

"I am, gotdamn it!"

"Think about suckin' my dick while you cum."

"You want me to think about your big fuckin' dick? You want me to think about you cummin' in my dirty lil' mouth? Oh God, yesss! Yes! Yessss! Oh God, B, I'm cummin! Oooouuu-weeee, B! Gotdamn ittttt!" I squirted all over Shamarah's face for the first time ever.

"Bitch!" she exclaimed, not knowing how to respond to me doing that. I didn't know how to. I was too overwhelmed. I couldn't believe it happened. Shamarah ran to the bathroom to wash her face, still cussing me out as she did.

Meanwhile, I lay there breathing hard, trying to recover when I remembered Lil' B said he had some good news for me. I hoped he was impressed with the spur of the moment phone sex we'd just had. More importantly, I hoped we would be having sex in the near future so we can do all the things we'd just fantasized about doing to one another. I would let Lil' B fuck me in every hole in a heartbeat if he wanted to, and I wouldn't charge him a dime. I wonder was he telling the truth when he said he'd dreamed about me. I must be on his mind real heavy when he'd done that. What were his thoughts when he was thinking of me? Were they similar to what he'd just told me? I would love to be on my knees, looking up to him, with a mouth full of his dick.

"Hello? You still there?" I asked the silence on the phone.

"Yea, I'm still here. You straight now?" He chuckled.

"Oh, I'm good," I sighed. "Has your dick gone down yet?"

"It's still tryin' to, but it's gettin' there. You a real freak. You have no idea how close I was to pullin' out my dick and bustin' every damn where."

"You could have. I wanted you to. Maybe when you get home, you can bust your load while thinkin' of bustin' in my mouth, on my ass, tits, or wherever you like."

"Maybe I will. Anyway, back to why I called you. I talked to the producers on *Love N Da Hood* and got you an interview with them for a spot on the show. To be honest, you have the spot secured already as a favor to me. All I want you to do is make them know that you're no mistake, that you deserve to be on the show. Make America fall in love with you, no matter what you gotta do. You make social media get to tweetin' about you, and the role's in my movie is yours. I've even put the scenes you would play on hold until after this. You're not camera shy, are you?"

"Absolutely not. I'm an ex-stripper, remember? Have you seen my IG page? But I gotcha, B. I give you my word I won't let you down. And I thank you from the bottom of my heart for what you're doin' for me. Are you goin' to let me show you my appreciation and gratitude one day?" I had to ask. I wanted to do whatever I had to so he would know I was thankful.

"I doubt if we ever get around to dat. I be so busy."

"How about you make time for it?"

"If it happens, it happens. If not, a simple thank you is enough for me," Lil' B wasn't tripping on pussy like that. Ain't no telling how many bitches he was fucking that was finer than me.

"So, when do I get to meet the producers?" I was ready to meet them today if I had to. Unfortunately, they didn't want to meet with me until this coming Sunday at the same hotel I had chilled with Lil' B and his fam in. Only difference, this time, I would meet with the producers in the hotel's restaurant at 3 o'clock p.m. sharp.

"Don't be late, Nikki." Lil' B warned. I promised him I wouldn't. Shortly after, Shamarah walked in, asking me if I was still on the phone with Lil' B. I nodded my head, and she snatched my phone from me.

"Hey. B. Good to hear from you. Yea, I'm alright. How are you doin'? Don't you know this bitch squirted nut all in my face all in my eyes and shit? Tell me why I think it was piss and not cum."

"Hoe give my phone," I grabbed my phone back and could hear Lil' B laughing his motherfucking ass off! "Don't mind her, B. I'll talk to you later. Okay, bye." I hung up and told Shamarah the wonderful news of my new job, then returned the favor by eating her ass and pussy. I tried to get her to squirt like I had, but she couldn't. It's cool. She came twice and I swallowed it all.

******

Tia, Shamarah, Rachel, and I were out celebrating my newfound success. We were at this fancy restaurant in Bankhead called Hollywood's Legend. Tia had made the recommendation that we come, said it was a place she and the twins' dad used to frequent when they were together. This was her first time mentioning this to me. I asked her why she'd never brought me here before. She shrugged her shoulders, not giving a clear answer. I didn't press for one. It wasn't that serious. We walked inside, looking fabulous. Forget a dime, we were the whole dollar piece and every patron inside was about to find out. We all had on dresses that hugged our voluptuous bodies tight. Except for Rachel's no booty having ass. Cuz was still killing it though in a dress that matched her eyes. Shamarah wore a nude colored one that complemented her beautiful skin. Tia's red Michael Kors dress probably was the most expensive in the bunch. I was giving her a run for her money in my all white Christian Dior dress that displayed every curve I owned. When we walked inside, every head turned their attention to us. I took a moment to take it all in, even taking time to check out the place.

It was commendable, I give it that. I could tell that a lot of important people came through the place. I was no restaurant critic, but judging from the interior, I'd give it three and a half stars. I still had to taste the food to see what the place was really working with. Tia had done a ton of bragging on their fajitas and chicken salads. I couldn't wait to bite into a salad. The hostess walked up, greeted us, and showed us our table. The pretty hostess said we were lucky because the table had just become available. She seated us by a window. I rushed to sit by it on the strength that I liked to watch people come and go. About an hour and a half later, after eating our food and desserts, these bitches ordered them something to drink. Not I. I would be the designated driver tonight. Not long after their orders arrived, a very familiar face from my past walks up to our table.

"Nikki? Rachel?" He asked.

"Oh my god, Kahari. Heyyy!" I slid past Shamarah to give Kahari a hug. He was the guy that found me on the side of the road, the day Money had beat me half to death. "What are you doin' here?" I was in a state of amazement. I thought I would never see him again.

"I'm with my brother and his wife. Wassup, Rachel. How's it goin'?" Rachel finally stood up to give him a hug.

"Hey Kahari. It's been goin'. Long time, no see, Mister. How have you been?" Rachel asked, then returned to her seat.

"Tryna stay free. That's why I moved up here. Stayin' in Mississippi gon' get a nigga a life sentence. Either dat, or in somebody's graveyard," Kahari said. I took the opportunity to introduce him to Shamarah and Tia.

"This is our homeboy Kahari from Mississippi. Big ol' J's."

"You gotta know dat," he said as he, Rachel, and I formed the letter J with our hands, throwing them up high. It was something every Jacksonian did when representing our town.

I was happy to see Kahari. He was still handsome as ever. Tall, slim, with a whole lot of gasconade. For those of you who didn't know what that meant, it meant swagger. He had on some Balmain jeans from Paris with a white Polo V-neck, and some Versace Chain Reaction on his feet. The only jewelry he had on was a presidential Rolex. Made me wonder what kind of job he had. I looked at the girls and they were all checking him out.

"Mind if I steal Nikki away from y'all for a second or two?" he asked the girls.

"No. Go right ahead," answered Rachel. "And I hope this won't be the last time seeing you."

"Hopefully, it won't be," Kahari was looking at me when he spoke those words, making me feel some type of way. We went to the bar to talk.

"So, what are y'all gettin' into when y'all leave here?" he asked.

"I don't really know. Me and the girls just out celebratin'."

"Oh yea? What's the celebration?"

"I've been cast on this reality show called *Love N Da Hood*. You familiar with it?"

"Of course, I am. When I was locked up it was one of dem shows dat got a nigga head bust if he tried to turn the channel. It came on, on a Monday. I used to be watchin' it. But congratulations though. That's big. You must be really feelin' yourself?"

"You have no idea. I feel good about it. Nonetheless, I'm a little nervous at the same time."

"Why's dat?"

128

I went on to explain to him what Lil' B was doing for me. "Wait a minute! Hold up! You know Lil' B?" I smiled yes. "And you're going to star in one of his movies?"

I smiled again, this time showing more of my teeth. "Excuse me bartender." Kahari said. The bald black man walked up, offering his service. I was about to tell Kahari that I didn't drink when he asked the man for a pen and piece of paper. "A napkin will do if you don't have a piece of paper." Kahari said.

The bartender handed him a pen and napkin and Kahari handed both items to me. I was confused.

"If you haven't already signed one, I want to be the first one to get your autograph."

"Awww!" I know my face turned crimson from the blushing I was doing. That was by far the sweetest gesture any man has ever made to me. It caused a chill to run down my spine. I took the items and signed, "To my very first fan, Kahari. Much love from Nikki Bunz!"

He looked at the napkin. Now he was confused. "Nikki Bunz?"

"Bunz comes from the size of my ass," I said, as I gave him the short story of how I became a stripper, urban model, ex-convict, and now a reality star. I called myself a star already because sometimes you had to speak things into existence. Kahari was completely surprised to learn that I'd been to prison. I explained to him the reason, telling him about me being on probation and all.

"You don't play, do you?"

"Just when it comes to someone fuckin' over me will I get on some gangsta shit. Enough about me for now. Tell me what you been up to. Start with what happened to you and why I never heard from you again when you went to prison. You know how many days I ran to the mailbox, hopin' I'd gotten a letter from you?" I declared. "The letdown was real."

"My bad about dat, Jew."

Ah hell, there goes that Jew word. How could I forget it? It has nothing to do with religion. It was a term that people from my hometown use in their slang. I hadn't heard it in a long time. Any who, Kahari continued explaining himself.

"I didn't want to be a distraction in your life. I thought it would be the best if I didn't bring you into dat world. You didn't know then, but now you know dat prison is very challenging to your mental and emotional capacity."

I nodded my head. After serving time myself, I could feel where he was coming from. Prison had indeed been very challenging to me physically, especially when the bitches found out I used to model. One of them hoes got an issue of a magazine I was in and showed everybody. All hell broke loose then. I doubt if Kahari had to endure what I had to as far as the rapes, bullying, and all the other bullshit. Oh, well. It is what it is. So happy that all of that is behind me now.

Time passed faster than I wanted it to. I was enjoying Kahari's and I conversation when the girls walked up pointing out that it was getting late. I wanted to invite Kahari back to my place, but I didn't want him to look at me in a degrading manner. I loved the way his eyes lit up when he looked at me. Even back when we first met, he looked at me with so much personal interest, adoration, affection, respect, and all those things that lets a woman know that a man had a desire to be with her. I loved the attention he used to give me. Tonight was no different. Oh yes there was. I was ashamed of who I was. If he ever caught wind of the whore I am, even though I get paid to be one, I was afraid he would put distance in between us as far as the east is to the west. If it were any other dude, I wouldn't care. Kahari and I exchanged numbers and when I made it home, after my shower, we exchanged texts for an hour before he finally called.

"Took you long enough," I said. "I was beginning to think that you were scared to call."

"That was my brother's doing. We went to a club so that's why. My bad, it won't happen again."

I was on the other end, smiling from ear to ear. Instead of him being in the club trying to get with other bitches, he spent all of his time texting with me. Major points on his behalf. We talked all night. I don't remember falling asleep on him. For some apparent reason, I woke feeling joyful as ever. Hmmm. I wonder why. Just playing. I felt like that because of Kahari. He had a unique way in making me feel special. Was I in love with him already? That was a good question to think on. All I knew was that I felt damn good.

Zion

Chapter Seventeen

I arrived thirty minutes early to my meeting with the producers of *Love N Da Hood*. Kahari said that if I showed up beforehand, it would show them that I was serious and focused. He had accompanied me here today and was waiting on me in the lobby while I handled my business. The producers were indeed impressed that I hadn't arrived late. There were four of them, two men and two women. One man was white but the other three were black. They all looked to be in their early to mid-fifties. I shook each of their hands, greeting them all with, "Good afternoon."

When I shook the light-skinned woman's hand, she said, "Judging from your body alone, America's going to have a hard time keeping their eyes off of you," Of course she reminded me how I resembled Kylie Jenner.

"I was going to say that, too," Said the Hershey black woman, hair full of gray dreadlocks.

"So was I," the white man chimed in. Not a second later, along came the black man with his opinion.

We took or seats and the light-skinned woman introduced herself as Pamela. She was one of the creators of the show and was also an executive producer. The black man was her husband, his name's Vincent. He was the co-creator and an executive producer as well. The other two were associate producers. They were all friends that made a boatload of money together. They seemed like nice people. I liked the vibes they were giving off. Pamela wanted to know if I was a fan of their show, if so, who did I like the most, and why. I liked R&B singer, Chivonne and her husband, Tristen. I liked them the most because they kept it the realest. They didn't sugarcoat anything. If they were asked how they felt about something, they were giving it to you live and direct, no filters at all. They were the boss couple of the show. Chivonne beautiful and Tristen's the finest man on the show. Whenever I would watch *Love N Da Hood*, I would fantasize about having a threesome with them. I was excited to meet them whenever that would be.

"We've heard that you went to prison for arson," Pamela said.

"Yes, I have. That's not a problem is it?"

"No not at all. In fact, we want to build your story around it. We want the people of America to see you as an independent woman who has survived prison and now gets out to pursue her modeling career. We wanna introduce you as an urban model, if that's okay with you."

"It just sounds a lot like my life," I said.

"Exactly," Vincent added. "That's the whole point of it all. We want this to be as real as possible. It's good for TV. We have a storyline already written up for you. It's going to be the perfect drama to bring to the show."

"Drama?" I blurted out. Ah hell, I had to play a drama queen. I thought they had plenty of people on the show to play drama queens and kings. I didn't want people to see me for the girl who was always with some drama. But hey, if that's what they wanted, then that's what they were going to get from me. "I won't have to come between Chivonne and Tristen, will I?" I asked, not down with doing that.

"That won't be the case, so you don't have to worry about it. It's not in the script." Pamela assured me.

Script? I thought everything flowed freely. That's the point of it being "reality" isn't it? Who was I to call them out on it? Whatever's good for TV and gets you the viewers, go with what's working.

"Okay. I'm down for whatever. I just have one question," I said.

"Ask it," said Pamela.

"You guys seem to know an awful lot about me. How is that so?"

Pamela smiled, explaining how she had her ways of knowing people's personal lives. All I was thinking from that point was being on TV and completing the mission Lil' B assigned me to. They could know my social security number, I wouldn't care. I looked at this as a business and nothing else. Pamela said that there was more.

"More like what?"

They all looked at each other in a peculiar way. Ah shit. Some bullshit was going on, I could feel it.

"We'd like you to come to our suite with us," Pamela exhorted.

Instantly, I thought I would have to have sex with them from the way they were acting. Old freaks. I heard stories about how rich people have orgies and sex games to initiate people into their circles and pacts. Was this the sacrifice I had to take? Would I have to suck these old men shriveled up dicks? Did the women's pussies still get wet? Damn you, Lil' B! He didn't tell me I had to do all of this. Was I down with it? Absolutely. I told them okay, and we walked out of the restaurant. I stopped to tell Kahari he could leave on account of I didn't know how long I would be. I told him I would call an Uber. Pamela overheard me telling him and said he could come up too. I looked nervous, considering if I was about to commit myself to an all-out orgy, I didn't want Kahari to know. Maybe I was overthinking and misreading Pamela and them. I decided to take a chance on that being the case, that I was tripping, and we went on up to their suite. We walked inside and there were a lot of people there. Y'all already know I was thinking that it was indeed an orgy. The only thing was, they had on their clothes and there were four big ass white dudes wearing black shirts with Security stenciled on the front and backs of them.

"Oh hell, fuck nah!" I heard someone say. I looked to my left to see who it was and there was Yasmin and Alisa both standing up, protesting my presence. "What is she doin' here?!" Yasmin asked, yelling like she was outside.

I wanted to run over and punch her and Alisa in their damn faces. I couldn't stand them hoes. I knew why I was here. A better question was, what the hell were they doing here? In the interest of us about to fight, security had to stand between us. We were exchanging fuck you's, kiss my asses, suck a dead dog's dicks, bitch, I'll kill you's, and hope your mama dies! Anything that would make the other madder than we already were.

"Ladies! Are you guys finished? We do need to discuss business, being that it's the reason I called you all here. I know at least one of you wants to make some money, am I correct?" Pamela took control of the room.

"What's going on Pam?" Yasmin asked.

I forgot she used to be on the show for the first two seasons. *Love N Da Hood* was entering its fifth season. Anyway, Pamela had us sit down and listen to her. She wouldn't speak another word until we sat our asses down. She clarified why she wanted us all here. She wanted Yasmin back on the show. Yasmin had only left the show to pursue better opportunities, which never panned out for her. Alisa had made a few guest appearances here and there. Pamela thought it would be the perfect storyline if we all came on the show to glamourize our real-life drama for the world to see. She said it would boost the ratings back to where she needed them to be. According to her, the show had taken a slight decline in viewer's ratings.

"Are you out of your mind?" Alisa bellowed. "I won't do it. I'm not puttin' my personal business out there for people to see me like that. Ungh-ungh, no way."

"What's the matter? Afraid people will see the dog ass bitch you really are and the fuckery you pulled on me? You don't want them to know that I was victimized?" I screamed again.

"Bitch, fuck you, okay? You weren't a victim of a damn thang! Yo' ass wanted what Cali and I put on you. Don't deny it!"

"That's so not the point. The point is, is that you lied to me. Just admit it."

"I won't admit to shit. You got what you wanted."

"No, I didn't. I was supposed to be on the cover like you promised. You said if I fucked you and Cali, I would get the cover," I said, not caring that I was telling our business to everybody there, including Kahari. I was so mad. I didn't care what he thought of me at that point.

"It wasn't her call to make. That was my call. I make all the final decisions." Yasmin finally said something.

"What the fuck ever!" I scoffed. Man, I wanted to beat these bitches to death, that was how mad I was at them.

"Now somebody tell me how this doesn't make for a great show." Vincent said.

"I'm not doin' it," Alisa held her ground.

"Yas?" Pamela looked at Yasmin.

"I'm in."

Alisa peered at her sister in disgust. "Don't you dare look at me like that. You know damn well I need the money, after all the debt I got put in tryin' to relocate my business to Memphis. Don't act like none of this is your fault."

"Oh God, there you go bringin' that shit up again."

"And? It's the truth," Yasmin yelled.

"I'm out of here." Alisa stood to leave. Pamela told her that she may want to hear their offer before walking out.

"Lisa, you owe me this. Now sit your ass back down!"

"Woof-woof! Better listen to your master, bitch!" I made fun of Alisa as she returned to her seat.

"Shut the fuck up!" Yasmin said to me. I was still laughing. I gave her the middle finger to talk to.

Pamela gave each of us a piece of paper with the amount of money we'd make for each episode. I was satisfied with the amount they were offering me. I knew they would make more than me. I didn't care. There was an end game in it for me and I'd be making way more money than the two of them put together. After we looked at our numbers, we were given waivers to sign. We couldn't file any lawsuits on *Love N Da Hood* if we got into a physical altercation with anybody and hurt ourselves while filming episodes. They wouldn't be liable for any of our medical bills. I thought that was some bullshit since they wanted us to be with all this drama every damn episode. It was highly likely that I would go upside one of their heads. I read over everything before signing. So did Yasmin and Alisa. There was an incentive in the contract stipulating that if the show reached a specific number of viewers, then we would be given more money. Pamela said that they would start shooting the first episode in three more weeks. They were negotiating the location. She advised us to get our fans and followers involved to get them ready for the season's premiere. We were all in agreement before we left. Pamela couldn't trust us to make it out of the hotel in one piece, so she had her security team to escort us out. Luckily, Yasmin and Alisa were parked on the other side of the hotel. When Kahari and I made it to his Chevy Silverado, he asked me if I was ready to be a star.

"Is the hair on my head red?"

"And you know dis!" We laughed as he held the door open for me.

This man was one of a kind. One like I had never met before. He was so sweet to me. I like the way he paid attention to detail, and to me. He wasn't pressed for sex. He hadn't even tried to have sex with me yet nor had he tried to spend the night at my place. Most guys begged me to have sex with them, to take me to their homes or come stay the night at mines, but not Kahari. He was on a different level.

Last night, he took me to a concert by The Weeknd, and after walking me to my door, we kissed like soulmates. I could feel the love he had for me in his kiss. I know he could feel that my love for him was mutual. He wrapped his arms around me, pulling me in closer. My nipples were hard because I was turned on. Pussy was sopping wet. I wanted him to take me inside and fuck my brains out, make me crazy for him. In place of, he told me he would call me when he made it home. What the hell! He didn't want this tight pussy of mine. I couldn't believe it. I know he wanted to by the way he kissed me. What was I missing? I hoped to find that out the next time we were together.

He closed the door of his truck smiling that adorable smile of his. God, I wanted him. I thought about taking him right here in the parking lot, but I didn't want to risk going to jail. It was alright, I would wait until it was the perfect time to make my move. When he got in the truck, he kissed me. He was definitely making me feel some type of way about him.

Zion

Chapter Eighteen

"Hold up. Say that again. You're what?"

"You heard me. I'm in love with Kahari."

"Bitch, it's only been three days."

"No, it's not. I've already told you how the two of us met, so the chemistry's always been there to begin with. But that's beside the point. Is there a law sayin' we have a certain amount of time to fall in love? No. Does the heart sometimes want what it wants? Yes, and there's not a damn thing we can do about it when that happens. Since Kahari's been back in my life, he's all I've been thinkin' about. He's all I want."

"More than being on TV and potentially co-starring in a movie?"

"Yes! You'd think by me being who I am, that I would be more focused on fame, but I'm not."

Tia and I were at my place having a conversation about my feelings towards Kahari. She thought I was moving incredibly fast, telling me that love didn't work that way. I had to remind her that she'd been in love twice before. The only reason I was talking to her to begin with, I thought she'd be able to relate to where I was coming from. Instead, she was giving me pushback, telling me to ignore my feelings, how I should put up a wall, anything that would reject my heart from what it wanted.

She went to talking gibberish to me, saying stupid shit like, "The heart can be selfish sometimes. Most people would tell you to follow your heart. That's not always good because like you just said, the heart wants what it wants, right? How selfish and greedy does that sound to you? Following your heart can sometimes lead you down the wrong roads in life. I'll give you an example. Hear me out. Let's say your heart is tellin' you to eat your favorite food, but the doctors have already warned you not to, your favorite food is bad for you, and can even run your blood pressure sky high, and cause you to have a heart attack or stroke. But your heart is tellin' you to go ahead and eat it 'cause the heart wants what it wants even after knowin' that your favorite food can potentially cause you death. What do you do in that situation? Give in to the heart and take risks of a lifetime of unhealthy livin'? Or do you take the commonsense approach and do what's best for you?"

I thought that was a terrible analogy she used. Be that as it may, I felt where she was coming from. However, my heart wanted to feel for Kahari. Up until now, I had never been in love before. It felt great to be in love, fascinating even. Most of all, I felt human. All my life I thought sex was the key to a man's heart. After all the sex I had, where the hell was my man? I didn't have one. On account of my past, none of them wanted to be a real man to me because of the woman I was. Who would want to take home a stripper? Whore? Prostitute? A slick sex addict? What man in his right frame of mind would want to introduce me to their families and would want to spend the rest of their lives with a bitch like me? None. Nada. Zero. Zilch. Not one freakin' soul. Those kinds of men were nonexistent. They didn't live in the world I did.

I felt where Tia was coming from as a friend, trying to give me a sanctuary from a broken heart. She told me how a broken heart can damage the soul. All in all, she wanted me to be sure that this was what I wanted. Most certainly, it was. Without a question. No ifs, ands, or buts. I wanted to love Kahari. He made me want to be a better person. I may just have to go by the name, Karolina with a K. Hell nah! Nikki Bunz will reign supreme forever!

"I see Evan's bought you a new necklace," I said, trying to change the subject.

"Okay, Nikki. Don't say I didn't warn you," Tia picked up on my tactics. "I'm not goin' to preach about it. You a grown woman. You know what's best for you."

I was about to tell her she didn't have to say it like that, but a knock at the door prevented me. I opened the door and standing there smiling was my man, Kahari Smith. He had a surprise lunch for me in hand. He was so thoughtful, always making me feel significant.

"Come in babe," I said, after giving him my lips to kiss the flavor off them. He walked in, speaking to Tia.

"'Sup, Tia? If I knew you were here, I woulda brought you somethin', too."

"I already ate. How you are doin' Kahari. I'm surprised you remember my name."

"I try to be good with names," Kahari said as I took the Burger King's bags and drinks out of his hands, heading to the kitchen. I told him I was a sucker for the Whopper.

"We were just talkin' about you," Tia confessed.

"Good or bad?"

"A little bit of both."

"I assume all the bad came from you?"

"It wasn't bad like I was sittin' up in here sayin' bad things about you when I don't know nothin' about you at all."

"Right."

"Nikki's my little sister. I'm just tryin' to protect her from movin' too fast if you know what I mean?"

Kahari finally sat down on the sofa. "I feel you, Tia. Niggas out here crazy these days. You don't want her mixed up with none of them, especially on a level like dat. It's good she has someone tryin' to protect her," He turned his attention to me. "The thing about me I won't let her move too fast. I'm a patient man."

That, he was. He still hadn't attempted to have sex with me. I guess I would just have to throw the pussy at him if he kept that up. Looking back to Tia, he continued, "She has two people who care about her and will protect her always. I was protectin' her when I first met her."

"She's told me the story. But, duly noted that you'll be protectin' her best interests as well. You seem like a nice guy with good intentions. I don't know. Too early to really tell right now. Just know that I'm watchin' you," Tia used her fingers to point from her eyes to his, causing us all to laugh. "Well, I'm about to roll out. I got thangs to do. Y'all have fun and enjoy your lunch date. I'll call you later, Nikki."

"Alright. Lock the door on your way out." Before Tia left, she peered at Kahari, reminding him that she wasn't playing when she said would be watching him, and she walked out the door.

"She's a trip," I said, biting into my Whopper.

"She loves you and wants what's best for you," Kahari replied, walking over to take a seat across from me at the kitchen's table.

I passed him his chicken sandwich and we ate and talked like the newly lovebirds we were. What impressed me about him was the fact that he never brought up me having a threesome with Alisa and Cali. It had been a week now and he still hadn't brought it up. Afterwards, we went to sit on the couch, and I turned on the TV.

"What you got planned for today?" I asked him. He looked at his watch.

"I got a few things to take care of in a few hours. I thought I'd chill with my baby until then."

"Oh, I'm your baby?" I smiled, propping my legs across his lap.

"Been my baby."

144

"Can I ask you somethin' since I'm your baby?"

"I'm listenin'." I asked him why he hadn't tried to have sex with me yet when I'd made it very clear that I wanted him.

He sighed deeply, saying that he didn't want me to feel like I was pressured into having sex with him. I responded that I didn't feel like that at all.

"It's certainly not the case. So, what's the real reason?" I pressed.

"Nikki, I'm a street nigga. I'll forever be one. Some things just don't change. Remember we were talkin' the night I ran across you at the restaurant and you made it clear dat you have no interest in datin' dat kind of dude? You said you were scared to go out with dudes like dat. I'm dat dude, Nikki. I sell drugs. I tote big pistols, own choppas and Ak's. I shoot 'em too, whenever it's necessary. If it comes down to it, I won't hesitate to protect my life. I am the streets. So, I didn't want to get our feelings involved and get you to do somethin' dat you're against. I respect you way too much. Do I like you? Hell yes! Do I have deep feelings for you? Hell yes! But-"

I stopped him right there by jumping in his lap to give him the most passionate tongue kiss I'd ever given before. To hell with what I said about never dating a street dude again. People had the right to change their minds whenever they wanted. I wasn't about to let some standard or rule I made keep me from happiness. I couldn't see me selling myself short like that. I was adding an exception to my commandment because Kahari made me happy. I was tonguing him down when he pulled his head back.

"Bae, your breath smell like dem stinky onions you were eatin'. I'm straight on yo' kisses.'' He laughed, turning his head.

"Ha-ha-ha! Whatever. You gon' give me some kisses," I kissed him all over the side of his face, blowing my onion smelling breath in his nose. We were killing ourselves laughing.

"You act like you're ready for me," he said, following the laughter.

"More than ready." I said, feeling him hardening beneath me. Instinctively, I grinded my hips. "What's that I feel right there?"

"You know exactly what dat is."

"Feels like someone is ready for me."

"Been ready for you."

"How about you come show me how ready you are?"

He stood up with me. I wrapped my legs around his waist as he walked to my bedroom. I was kissing his neck, his lips, and ear before he laid me down on my bed and started kissing me softly from my lips to my neck. I swear no man had ever done me like him. I knew for a fact Kahari loved me. Those deep feelings he said he had for me was none other than love. He was too thugged out to tell me. It was okay, though. Actions spoke louder than words any day of the week. He paused to remove my Atlanta Falcons shirt. I unclasped my Victoria' secret bra, revealing my double D's. He grabbed them both, squeezing them as he suckled on my right nipple. He pinched my left one, making me gasp. He licked my nipple with a gentle touch while pinching harder on the other one.

"Ohhh!" I arched my back, grabbing his head as my clit throbbed and swelled. He bit down hard on my nipple. Pain. A moment later, he was sucking it gently again. Pleasure. I dug my hands into his scalp as he took turns with my breasts. He started kissing his way down my body. I felt the tip of his heated and damp tongue circling my navel. He was in uncharted territory. My clit throbbed repeatedly. Good gracious, I was horny for him. His hands found the seam of my matching Atlanta Falcons cheerleading shorts and he tugged them off. He glared at my pussy, licking his lips in apprehension. I spread my legs wider, placing a hand over my hairless pussy. I spread the folds, inserting a finger inside of me. His eyes were glazed with shameless lust. I slowly pumped my finger back and forth.

"Mmmmmm. I can't wait to feel you inside of me," I pumped faster, making squishing sounds.

Kahari pulled his shirt over his head, then unbuckled his belt. I couldn't wait to see his package. Was it long and thick? Long and skinny? I couldn't imagine it being small. I pumped my finger faster and faster as he pulled his boxers and pants down. He kicked off his shoes before standing upright. Oh my gosh! All that meat pointing at me, looking incredibly bold and beautiful. Powerful. Determined. Ready to fuck me into a mental blankness. I withdrew my finger and began sucking on it, wishing it were his dick I was sucking my cream from. Seeing me do that, Kahari climbed into bed with me.

"Scoot up," he said.

I slid up, head inches from the headboard. Kahari positioned his face square with my vagina as I spread my pussy lips open for him. My clit stood up proudly, ready for whatever. Seconds passed when Kahari blew his breath on my bud for a short period of time before kissing and sucking on the fingers that had been inside of me.

"You like the way I taste?"

He sucked all my juices from my fingers then licked all around my hotbox, everywhere except for where I wanted to feel his tongue the most.

"Please, Kahari. Don't tease me, baby. Lick meee!" Hunger pounded at my clit. His hands pressed beneath my thighs, pushing my legs back. Nothing but pussy in his face as he worked his tongue from my pussy-hole to my clit. He swiped his tongue left. Again. Then right. Again. Up. Down.

He traced the letter K on my clit, followed by, A, H, A, R, and I, conquering his new territory. Afterwards, he put his whole mouth over my clit and breathed on it like he was trying to fog up a window. Desperation captured my cries of pleasure. My mouth opened wide as the silent sounds escaped. I've never in my life felt a sensation quite as good as the one Kahari was administering to me. When words did become available for me, I cried out ones I couldn't comprehend. I didn't know what the hell I was saying while my orgasm took hold of me. My juices gushed on his tongue and he lapped it all up, greedy for more.

"Kahari, please fuck me now! Please!" I wailed, when I came back to my senses. He got on his knees, putting on a Magnum. He placed the folds of my legs on his shoulders, entering me in one long stroke.

"Ooouuu!"

"Open your eyes," he whispered.

I opened them, wrapping my arms around his neck. We gazed into each other's eyes as he thrust his hips unhurried, gradually filling me up with his long cock. He pulled back until only the tip was in me. Aiming it left, he pushed down strong against my walls causing another feeling I never felt before. Kahari wasn't fucking me. He was making tender, sweet love to me and he wanted me to watch him do so. I pulled his head down so I could moan into his mouth. His hips circled left recurrently.

"Babyyy! Why me? Whyyy!"

"Why what?" He grunted, repeating his delivery.

"Why you makin' me feel-ohhhh, God!"

"Feel what? How am I makin' you feel?" He thrust again and again, daring me to tell him what he was doing to me.

"You're...mmmmm...makin' me feel loved, Baby! I've never felt-oh shit-like thisss...Ooouuu, ye-yessss-mmmngh!" I felt the tears falling out the side of my eyes.

"Is dat why you're cryin'?"

I nodded my head up and down, as I broke into a sob. I couldn't believe I was crying. They said good loving will make you cry sometimes. Kahari was affectionate, kissing away my tears. It was at that moment I realized that I would love him for the rest of my life. Regardless of what happened between us, he would always hold a special place in my heart.

"Kahari?"

"Wassup, Bae?" We were still gloating one another. He was remarkably handsome, one of the realest men I've ever met. I didn't care how long he's been in my life. I didn't care who had something to say about it or how they would judge me. This is my life. No one had to live it but me.

"I love you." He needed to know that I wanted to be his woman.

"Karolina, I've always loved you. I'm never lettin' you go again. Never!" He promised, as he pushed inside of me deeper. More sensual. More loving. He kissed me with the same energy he was making love to me with.

In the moment of us kissing, I reached down and pulled his rubber off. I had to feel him. It had been so long since I had unprotected sex. I never had it once in my adult life. Not one single time. I guided him back into my warmness and let him finish making love to me. I know we did our thang for close to an hour. He came inside of me twice. I'm not going to lie, I hoped I would be pregnant by the end of the week.

We took a shower afterwards, because he had to go and handle that business he had mentioned earlier.

"Are you comin' back?" I asked, sounding like I was hooked. Hell, truthfully, I was. Damn shame he had dick that good.

"As soon as I'm done." He glanced at his watch, stating that it would be another two to three hours before he returned.

When he did, he brought me some food from Hollywood's Legend. Damn, them was some good ass ribs. I wanted to punch the wall. We talked later after we ate and Kahari told me he was the Brickman, meaning, he pushed kilos of cocaine. He was into a little bit of everything. Molly, ice, spice, weed, xans. You name it, he sold it. He even had a connection where he sold guns. We talked about me moving in with him, but I talked him out of it when I told him about my P.O. and that I needed to maintain a low-profile.

"Fuckin' with her, I gotta lay low and play slow. Don't need her findin' out about you, because she'll try to use that to send me back to prison."

I broke it down to him. Honestly, I didn't want to be around any guns. I didn't like them. They scared me. I reasoned with him, saying that we would take turns spending nights at each other's place. He respected it. When the thought popped up, I dismissed the notion of telling him my past. I finally told him the situation with Alisa and Cali and how Yasmin was involved. I told him a lot more about me except all the men and women that paid me to have sex with them. He did ask me had I ever had sex with any of the patrons from the club and I lied like I hadn't. I felt bad for lying to him when he was giving me the chance to be truthful. Some things aren't meant to be told. I'm just being real.

Thereafter, we took a shower where I wasted no time dropping to my knees to suck his big dick while the water hit me in my face. I sucked him hard, pumping the base with my fist as my other hand toyed with my pussy. It didn't take long for him to cum in my mouth. I swallowed it all. We didn't make love that night. In place of, we sucked and fucked each other until the sun came up. Before going to sleep, I reminded my man that I loved him. Holding me tight, He reminded me of the same. That was all that matters. Anybody got a problem with it. You know what you can do. Go fuck yourself. It is what it is!

Zion

Chapter Nineteen

A week prior to *Love N Da Hood* shooting their first scene with me, I decided to drop a surprised visit in on my P.O. I was going to give her an update on my job change since I hadn't talked with her about me being on the show. I'd told so many other people, including my parents that I was about to be a reality star. My mom was happy for me. She knew about reality TV. Her favorite show was *The Real Housewives of Beverly Hills*. She never missed an episode. She was more than happy to know that I wasn't stripping anymore. I'd always kept it 100 with my mother and she'd always kept it the same with me. She never told my father about me stripping. He wouldn't understand nor accept that his little princess was dirty dancing for horny rich men and women of Atlanta and selling my body to them for their own sexual gratification. I probably danced or had sex with his favorite athlete. My father would've been highly disappointed with me if he knew that. It was bad enough he learned that I used to model in swimsuits and sexy lingerie for perverted magazines. The day he called to confront me, we exchanged some heated words about it, but over the years and with me doing time, he eventually came around to accept it. He said that despite his anger towards my modeling that he was proud of me for standing up for myself, for not letting anyone mess over me in any way they felt. He told me he loved me and will always no matter the profession I chose. Still, I didn't have the guts to tell him I was a stripper. He was happy that I had been casted on *Love N Da Hood*. Although reality TV wasn't his thing, he promised to watch a few episodes of me whenever the show came on.

I lit up social media on everybody's timeline I could think of, promoting my being on the show. For the most part, I got a ton of support. There was some backlash from the haters, which I expected. Nevertheless, I didn't pay it any mind. There were a few comments posted about Yasmin and Alisa about how they were going to beat me up if they saw me in the streets. That struck me as mildly odd. This was the first time someone's commented on my beef with them bitches. It had to be either Yasmin or Alisa, I thought. Fuck 'em! I kept on scrolling. I knew how to eat beef if I had to. Anyway, I parked outside of Ms. Taylor's office, not really paying attention to my surroundings. I was too busy texting Kahari a message letting him know I arrived. Not because I had to, it was because I wanted to.

I got out of my car and made it to the glass door. Just as I was about to open it, I noticed that the door was locked with a sign saying, out for lunch. I looked at my phone for the time. *Rather late for lunch,* I thought. Maybe she had been busy all morning and had to take a late one. I returned to my car to wait a few minutes for her to arrive. I hoped it was soon because I was only giving her ten minutes tops. If she didn't come back within those minutes, I would call her and schedule an appointment. I was sitting in my car, A.C. blowing while I went on IG. Three minutes must've passed before I looked up.

What. In. The. Hell? Son of a bitch! So that's how she found out about me being a stripper. My P.O. and Evan were standing on the other side of the door kissing and hugging. Two of his bodyguards stood close by. How? When did this happen? I was stunned. Hold up, that was an understatement. This shit hit me like a ton of bricks. I was paralyzed in amazement watching them tongue each other down. They had to have been fucking in there. What other reason would she lock the doors and put a sign up? I immediately turned on my phone's camera on record. I got their dog asses right where I wanted them. I was going to work out a deal with TMZ to see how much money I could get paid for this. Evan's bitch ass should've been more careful. Sorry Tia, but your man was playing with fire and it was time that he got burned. I let him make it too many times. They said Karma's a motherfuckin' bitch. This time her name's, Nikki. Not only was I going to TMZ, but I was also going to Dish Nation, People and Time magazine, US magazine, the local newspaper, and all of Atlanta's news stations. I was going everywhere I possibly could to bring Evan down from his high horse. Ms. Taylor was about to get caught up in the middle of my revenge. I didn't care. I had no sympathy for her. She should've been down with the winning team. I hope when shit hits the fan that her superiors fire her crooked ass.

I recorded Evan palming her lil' perfect booty, while she unlocked the doors. Oh, it got even better. After she kissed Evan goodbye, she did the same with his two bodyguards. OMG! Ms. Taylor was a complete freak. Apparently, they'd run a train on her, or they'd all participated in a foursome. It was hard to tell. Did she take a cock in her mouth, one in her pussy, and the other one in her ass at the same time? I wondered did she swallow their cum. Did they have her on her knees as they stood over her busting their loads on her face and boobs? Look at my freaky ass getting all off the mission. Let me concentrate on the real matter at hand. When Evan and his bodyguards walked out, I slouched in my seat so I wouldn't be seen. I managed to keep my phone at an angle that captured perfect images of all of their faces. I made sure to get a good shot of Evan's Maybach and tag number. I had his ass. I watched them leave the premises, then I saved the video to my phone. I sent a copy to Kahari, then called him to tell him what the video was for and not to share it with anybody. He couldn't stop laughing when I told him what I was using the video for. He had my back though, encouraging me to do my thang, because there was more that I was about to do. I hung up with him and walked pompously into Ms. Taylor's office. I was surprised to see her secretary or whatever the hell the woman was labeled. I shook my head. They'd been having a blast in here, hadn't they? Ms. Taylor welcomed me in her office. I could sense her attitude off bat. Not long ago, she was all happy go-go, probably taking all the dick she could stand.

"Good afternoon, Ms. Musgraves. How can I help you?" she said.

"I was droppin' by to tell you that I have a new job," I went into detail about the show.

"That's wonderful. I'm happy to hear that. Actually, I'm glad you stopped by. There is something that's been brought to my attention about you again. It happens to pertain to your boyfriend." Yep, Evan was dropping salt on me with my P.O. all because I wouldn't have sex with him. Petty motherfucker!

"What's my boyfriend have to do with anything?" I was curious about the information she had on Kahari.

"He's a convicted felon. And from what I hear, he's a convicted felon who's actively participating in drug activities. I hear that he has a few bodies under his belt. Is that true, Ms. Musgraves?"

"You heard all of this, or do you know this for a fact?

She looked at me, surprised that I was talking to her in the tone I was.

"It doesn't matter if I heard or know. What's important is that you have to end your relationship with him or-"

"You're goin' to send me back to prison. Yea-yea, whatever."

Ms. Taylor's eyes bucked wide. "Ms. Musgraves, need I remind you who you're talking to?"

"I thought I was talkin' to my probation's officer and not my mother. You're tellin' me who I can and can't have as a boyfriend, and I don't like it. You don't control my life," I exclaimed, heart pounding in my chest.

Ms. Taylor picked up the phone. "Susie, has Jimmy or Terrance made it back in yet? Neither one has. Okay, well whoever shows up first, have him come to my office. I have someone who needs to be transported to Fulton County Jail. Okay," she said, hanging up the phone. "Ms. Musgraves, I'ma need you to stand. I'm placing you in violation of your probation," she exclaimed, pulling out her handcuffs.

"You're sending me to jail?"

"Yes, I am."

"Before you do, I have a video of you on my phone that was just recorded before I walked in here. It's of you, Evan, and his bodyguards. Would you like to see it?" Ms. Taylor was looking like she'd seen a ghost.

"You're bluffing," She said, sitting back down.

"I think you know I'm not bluffin'." I played the video for her to see it. If she kept looking the way that she was, she was going to shit herself. She instantly picked up the phone to tell Susie to disregard her request, and then hung up. I had all the power up in this bitch. "I've sent a copy to my boyfriend that you were just speakin' on and my best friend. They have instructions of what to do with it if somehow, I go to jail. I'm sharin' this video for the world to see."

"Please, don't. You'll destroy my marriage, family, and career. Please." She pleaded with me.

I had to ask her what they were in here doing. My freaky side wouldn't let it go. Turns out, Evan and his bodyguards had been taking turns fucking the women. I figured that. I asked her where she and Evan had met. She said she ran into him at the Sprint Mart down the street from here. She stopped there every day after work to get her favorite chips. He'd approached her and just like many women had, she couldn't resist his celebrity status or charm. They started sleeping together days later.

"How could I not fall victim to his charm? He's Evan freaking Smith. The whole world knows who he is. Every woman wants to sleep with him."

"Not me," I told her how I thought that she'd been singled out by Evan. I also told her that after I refused to have sex with Evan because he was seeing my best friend, he began playing his little messy and childish ass games with me. I told her everything. Even the stalking like ways he'd shown.

"I know you're not lying about him probably singling me out. He did have an interest in you and your record, wanting me to be extra hard on you. He made up some story about how you'd messed over him one day when he was in town. He admitted to coming to the strip club you worked at and after a private show with you, you'd stolen his money. It was his idea that I make you quit. I'm so sorry," she sympathized with me.

"I'm sorry too. This is the only way to pay him back," I declared.

"Please, hear me out first. What if I can get you off probation for good? Would that be enough to make you reconsider?"

I mulled it over. "What about the restitution?" I asked.

"I have no control over that. You would have to take that up with the courts. I don't know anyone I can talk to about that. My guess is that you will have to pay."

"But you can get me off probation?"

"I can definitely do that." I thought it was well worth it. To be free from the fear of making the slightest mistake, would be the perfect relief for me.

"Don't tell Evan about this. If you do, then the deal's off about me going to the media."

"I promise you won't have to worry about that." She swore on God and her kids. She told me she would have my goldenseal in a week's time. I couldn't wait for that day to come. We shook hands, locking it in. To fuck with her, I asked her was she still going to see Evan. "To be honest with you, yes. I need that excitement that Evan provides for me. Don't get me wrong, I love my husband and my family. My husband is prudish when it comes to sex. He's just plain ol' missionary and that's it. I try to get him to spice things up. I want to be treated like a whore. I want to be fucked, not made love for a few minutes all the time. My husband doesn't even like for me to suck his dick. He has no idea how I love sucking dick. I have a fetish for it. I try to tell him, but his inhibitions won't listen. As pathetic as it may sound, I'm glad that Evan manipulated me. He brought excitement back to my life. He gives me what I want, what my body craves for. I need him in my life. However, I do hope that you pay him back some way that doesn't involve me." She laughed.

In the end, I had compassion for Ms. Taylor. I could feel her to a certain degree. What her man wouldn't do, another man will. The same way with men and their women. You know how that goes. Ms. Taylor told me she would call me in to sign my goldenseal. I would hold my video for insurance purposes in case she forgot our understanding.

As far as Evan was concerned, I was going to figure out a good way to pay his ass back. Most likely, it would affect Tia to some degree. But it was a chance I was willing to take. Tia didn't need Evan. He was no good and he was a cheater. He was a dog. It was time to put him on a leash. He needed to be punished for the petty shit he was on. It really didn't make any sense for him to be acting the way that he was. As I've said before, he's a multi-millionaire with all the money and fame in the world, and he was in his feelings because little ol' me, as unimportant as I was, wouldn't have sex with him. Tsk. Men. What a shame. I couldn't help but shake my damn head.

Chapter Twenty

The Philips Arena was jammed packed with thousands of people out representing with Lil' B for his birthday. I had never seen so many people come out to show their love and support the way they were for Lil' B. Family members, friends, loved ones, business associates, fans, celebs, professional athletes, and people Lil' B probably didn't know were in the building tonight, turning up with Lil' B for his 37th birthday. Guess who else was in the building? That's right, me and some of the cast members from *Love N Da Hood*. That included my favorite couple, Chivonne and Tristen, who I got a chance to meet and they were cooler and more down to earth in person than they were on TV. Not to mention, they both looked scrumptious. While we were talking, they had me fantasizing about having a threesome with them. Also, in attendance, was female rapper, The First Lady, who I also loved on the show, and last but not least, Yasmin and Alisa. Each of us had a cameraman and crew following us around for the night, filming season five's first episode. You know I had to be dressed phenomenal in a light blue Diane Von Furstenberg silk wrap snakeskin dress and white snakeskin H&M faux boots.

It was Lil' B's idea for us to shoot my first scene at his party after Pamela failed to reach a deal on the initial location. All in all, being at Lil' B's party couldn't help but boost the show's ratings, especially if he made a guest appearance in one of my scenes. The producers were using Lil' B's party as my introduction on the show. It would definitely help me if America saw that the two of us were connected. It would certainly raise more questions as to who I was. I was nervous only a snippet, but as the night progressed, so did my jitters. The storyline was Yasmin, Alisa, and I would coincidentally run into each other at the party and get into a heated argument and come close to throwing blows about me burning down Yasmin's business. Before that was to happen, I had to create my own buzz with some of the celebs in the house. It was to show that I was somebody who knew somebody. I still thought that if Lil' B and I were to mingle together, that would be good enough for the viewers.

In the meantime, I brought along my friends and loved ones. Kahari, his homeboy Black, Tia, Rachel, and Shamarah were enjoying the party like everyone else. They would be caught on camera here and there, but they weren't to be a part of the drama. It was my responsibility to remind them of that and to keep them at bay when my confrontation with Alisa and Yasmin went down. The producers would give the signal when it was time for the drama to unfold. Meanwhile, Cari Champion, the hostess of the night, introduced comedian, DC YoungFly to the stage to crack some jokes. He had everybody laughing at his crazy ass. He was by far, my favorite comedian. Dude was so funny. I loved watching him on Nick Cannon's *Wild-N-Out* show. DC YoungFly did a thirty-minute set, receiving a standing ovation for his performance. Afterwards Cari Champion introduced Lil' B and his I.S.M family to the stage. Cari told Lil' B happy birthday then she walked off stage with her sexy self, leaving Lil' B and his crew to perform.

All seven of them were given a mic and they set it off in that motherfucker. My girl, Josielyn Billups was on stage representing for the ladies, singing the hooks and rapping the songs she was featured on. They rapped a few songs they were on, then they finished their performance by rapping six of Lil' B's hit songs in honor of his special day. People in attendance were all rapping along with them, including myself, Kahari, and Black. After his epic performance Lil' B, his wife, and their bodyguards found me. I made sure that the cameras were rolling.

"What's good with you, Ms. Nikki Bunz?" he asked. I swear this man seemed to get more beautiful the more I saw him. I was acting all nonchalant in front of the cameras, like it was no big deal that one of HipHop's finest knew me.

"Happy birthday, old man," I laughed.

"Yea, right. You wish I were old. 'Preciate it, though. This here's my beautiful wife, Sunshine. Baby, dis the one I was tellin' you about who may get the role in my movie."

"Nice to meet you," I said.

"Pleasure's all mine," she replied.

Sunshine was a bad bitch. I had seen her on TV with Lil' B whenever he attended a red-carpet event. I'd also seen her in Time magazine on a picture with Lil' B and their kids. She was chocolate, beautiful, and incredibly sexy. But I got a bad vibe from her. She was looking at me with a slight frown on her face. I brushed it off as her being bougie or whatever you call rich people who have bad attitudes. I hated it when beautiful people had ugly attitudes. It made them hideous in my eyes, no matter how pretty or sexy they were. Sunshine definitely was high maintenance. I introduced Lil' B to Kahari, announcing him as my boyfriend. Then I introduced him to Tia, Rachel, and Black. I had to play it off with Shamarah. We all know the reason why. Speaking of which, I wondered where Ro was. I had seen him earlier, but he didn't see me. I made sure I dodged him when I saw his fine ass. I didn't want any drama. As soon as I thought about him, he and a woman I presumed was his baby's mother walked up with Head and his wife. Kahari and Lil' B were engaged in a conversation when Ro spoke. The exchange went rather smoothly, everyone acting as if it was our first-time meeting. Ro's and Head's girls were both cute, big booty sticking out their jeans and dresses. I caught Lil' B's wife still frowning at me. I started to say something to her.

"Why she's lookin' at you like that for?" Shamarah whispered in my ear.

I shrugged my shoulders. "I have no clue."

"She is acting like she wants to get beat up."

"Girl, hush. We do that and my career's over way before it even starts. Let her keep lookin' with her lookin' ass, as long as that's all she's doin'."

"I feel you. She probably wants to eat your pussy. That's the same look I had when I first saw you," Shamarah giggled.

"Hey, if that's what she wants to do, then all she gotta do is say it. I'll ride that pretty black face of hers all night."

As soon as we stopped laughing, my whole demeanor changed instantly. Evan's ol' bitch ass had walked up with his wife on his arms. He'd stopped to wish Lil' B a happy birthday. I looked at Tia who turned her head, gazing into the crowd. I turned back to Evan. It was only a matter of time before I wiped that conceited, holier-than-thou look from his face. I had a plan brewing in the pot for him. He made me think of Ms. Taylor. I was off papers now, so everything was a go now on getting my revenge on Evan. He was going to get what he deserved. I told Lil' B to enjoy the rest of his night, ignoring Evan and his skinny ass wife. No wonder he loved women with big booty's. I was about to walk away when Lil' B stopped me to introduce Evan and I. Although it was good publicity to have him present, I hated the ground he walked on.

"He's goin' to be starring in the movie, too," Lil' B declared.

Not if I had anything to do with it, he wouldn't be. I did some Oscar worthy acting when I fronted like it was my first-time meeting Evan, pretending like I was his biggest fan. I went as far as introducing him to my camp, Tia first of course. "Tia come meet the famous Evan Smith. You have all his movies girl," I could tell that Evan didn't like that at all. Despite so, he displayed his acting abilities by continuing to smile, and extending his hand for Tia to shake. What a performance. Tia knew that I was being messy. Talking to me through her teeth, she insisted that I cut it out. For the sake of her hurt feelings, I did. I knew she was upset about Evan's wife being in town. I stopped with my shenanigans and walked away with my camp in tow. We found a spot to party in and turned up with everybody else in Philips Arena.

After seeing me talking to Lil' B and Evan, people started coming over to introduce themselves, mainly they were being nosey, trying to figure out who I was since I had a whole camera crew following me around. They gave me props when they found out why there were cameras. A vast majority of them were fans of the show. Some knew me from Instagram and wanted autographs. A few celebs and athletes I slept with wanted to see what all the fuss was about concerning me. I was stealing the spotlight. When they approached, I made sure that off the bat, I made known Kahari and I's relationship status, so that neither of them would get any bright ideas about going home with me or me going someplace with them. I was letting them know that I was a changed woman. They respected it, and kept it moving.

Kahari seemed to be really enjoying himself. He stayed in the background, letting me get my shine on. He knew how important this night was to me. He didn't want to be seen on camera. He said he was straight on all that. On a few occasions, I saw him and Tia talking. Knowing him, he was telling her not to sweat Evan and his wife, advocating for her to enjoy her night. I could see the frown plastered all over Tia's face. She was heated. I knew she was ready to leave and

I wouldn't blame her if she did. Rachel and Black seemed to be hitting it off perfectly. They kept firing up blunt after blunt of loud, passing it back and forth between them and Kahari. Shamarah was stealing as much camera time as she could. For the most part, she stayed close to me. About thirty minutes later, I looked for Tia, and she was nowhere to be found. I asked Shamarah and Rachel had they seen her. Nope. Neither one had. I asked Kahari and Black. Same results. I texted her asking her whereabouts. As I waited for her reply, Kahari said that he had to leave because some very important business had come up.

"I gotta get on top of dis, Bae. I'll explain why later. Right now, I need to go run my bands up. I'll make it up to you when I make it home." Baby pulled me in for a kiss, gripping a handful of my booty. "In the meantime, you make sure you keep killin' dis night. Got me?" He asked kissing me some more.

"Mmmm. I gotcha, daddy. Be careful, okay?"

"Already."

"I love you," I couldn't help but tell him.

"Love you, too," he said, kissing me one last time, then he and Black made their exit.

Not long after, Pamela walked up. I didn't even know she was here. She came to inform me that my confrontation scene with Yasmin and Alisa was about to take place. "Are you ready?" she asked me.

"Let's get it," I said, feeling like a young Floyd Mayweather.

We were to bump into each other and relive the past. Now that I think about the past, I may slap the shit out of Alisa since Pamela advised us to make it look real as possible. How real would it be if I slapped her and snatched a chunk of her hair out of her head? It was all set up for us to meet up out of the patron's way so that we didn't mess around and hit one of them or spill our drinks on them. As soon as we got close, we went into a tirade of obscenities, kinda like the scene from the hotel. We had genuine hate for one another, so we didn't need to play like we did. Even Shamarah and Rachel jumped in to help me cuss them bitches out, although I had warned them not to. Shamarah went as far as swinging on Yasmin, even though she didn't lay hands on her. After our staged drama was over, before walking away, Yasmin and I exchanged more words with each other. She said she was going to get somebody to beat my ass.

"Why don't you do it yourself, scared bitch!" I dared her.

Pamela ended up liking Shamarah's and Rachel's depiction so much, she wanted to sign them on for a few episodes. Shamarah and Rachel were both ecstatic to hear that. They happily agreed and Pamela said she would have them to sign their contracts tomorrow morning. Pamela said they'd recorded enough footage for the night, so she rounded up her crew and they left. Rachel and Shamarah were so happy that they wanted to turn up for the rest of the night, even though we had an early morning breakfast scene to shoot for the follow up of what happened here tonight with Yasmin and Alisa. Rachel and Shamarah promised they would be up bright and early with me. I was happy to be sharing my success with them. I loved them so much. The highlight of my night was when Lil' B's wife approached me. Pulling me aside, she knocked me out with a bombshell.

"You know you remind him of someone. Has he told you that?" she asked me.

"Yes, he has. But he won't tell me who that someone is."

"She's someone who brought me some hard times in my life."

"I'm sorry to hear that."

"No need to be. The main thing is that she's gone now, and I don't have to worry about her ever again. Well, I thought I wouldn't have to until I saw you. Now I'm slightly worried again."

"You don't have to be. I'm nobody. Harmless. I'm just happy he's giving me an opportunity to be in his movie. I'll play a boot-shiner if I had to," I said, making her smile with my last comment.

"I'm sure you would. There's somethin' else I would like to ask you," she said.

"If it's havin' to worry about me, the answer is no. I'm not interested in him like that." I was lying through my teeth. I would fuck Lil' B if he ever made the move on me. Although I was lying, I thought I'd shut down any concerns of me trying to sleep with her husband.

"That's not what I wanted to ask you."

"Sorry. Me and my big mouth can't shut up sometimes. Go ahead and ask me."

She looked down at the floor for a moment before looking me square in my eyes. "How would you like to have a threesome with us?"

I started coughing. For whatever reason, I don't know why, her question threw me off guard for a brief moment. I peered at her, observing her posture. Oh my God, she was dead ass serious. I gave it some thought. I thought about Kahari. If she had asked me this question before Kahari came back into my life, I would've been all for it. I would've spent the night eating her pussy and sucking Lil' B's dick until they begged me to stop. Then, I would've acted out everything Lil' B and I fantasized about doing to one another during our phone sex conversation. But now that I was in love with Kahari, my perspective about a lot of things had changed. I wanted to be loyal to him like he had always been to me.

"Does Lil' B know about this?" I just had to ask. Maybe he was scared to ask me himself and sent his wife to do it.

"No, he doesn't. If you agree, trust me, it won't be too hard to get him on board."

I couldn't help but think about the vibe I'd mistaken as bad earlier. "I'm flattered, I really am. As much as I would love to eat you up, 'cause I know that pussy is just as pink as it wanna be with yo' chocolate self, I'ma have to decline." I said seeing disappointment on Sunshine's face.

"I can respect that. No pressure at all, Love. Well, enjoy the rest of your night. But do take my number in case you change your mind and wanna find out how pink my pussy really is. I'll let you in on a little secret. It's sweet as cotton candy as well."

Oh, my goodness, I was about to change my mind on the spot. I held tight to my morals and didn't. She gave me her number to save to my phone and walked off. Mmmm-mmngh, she had a nice, fat ass, throwing them thick hips of hers. I knew she was only trying to provoke me. I closed my eyes, knowing that if I didn't, I was going to call her back and tell her I'd reconsidered. When I opened my eyes back, she was gone. I returned to the fun with Shamarah and Rachel and we partied until the wee hours of the night. I looked at my phone and still hadn't received a reply text from Tia. I worried about her. I knew she was at home crying her eyes out. Poor Tia.

Zion

Chapter Twenty-One

It took a good minute, but I finally had Evan right where I wanted him. I paid a white dancer from Magic City handsomely to assist me in my plot for revenge. I couldn't use one from the Blue Flame because Tia had too many ties there. What I loved most about my plan is that the girl's name just happens to be, Kharma. What better way to pay back a no-good son of a bitch than with the person you're using to pay them back has the name Kharma. Her name had an H in it, but still, it was perfect. Kharma was indeed Evan's type. She was a definite head turner for sure. She was pretty with a mole on the right side of her nose, stood about five foot seven inches and had a booty that matched mine in size. The reason why I chose her to be a part of my scheme is the mere fact that she resembles me a smidge, only her hair is sandy blonde. I knew Evan wouldn't be able to resist a big booty white girl. It was hard for any black man to resist a white woman like that, and Evan was no different.

When I knew he was at Tia's, I had Kharma park her car beside his, faking like she was having car trouble. From what Kharma told me, Evan walked outside to find a damsel in distress, bent over under the hood of her car, wearing the tightest and shortest booty shorts Evan had ever seen. He had no choice but to notice her because she was on the side of his driver's door. In addition to that, he had no choice but to help her with her troubles. That happened a little over two weeks ago when part one of my plan had been achieved.

Today, Kharma and I sat in the back of Gladys Knight's restaurant where Kharma was about to show me part two of my plan. It would be the killer to Evan's career, marriage, and everything else that was important to him. Kharma passed me the phone I had given her to record them with. Let me warn y'all of how dirty I played the game. It may be unimaginable to some of you, sensitive to most perhaps. But revenge has no limits. Anything goes. Y'all know that. Kharma was to pretend that being raped was her ultimate fantasy, that it was the way she preferred to have sex, that feeling helpless and defenseless turned her own more than any other sex act. She expounded on how being totally powerless to a man was the thing that got her off the most.

"It took some real convincing to get him to have sex with me. He had a lot of reservations about it, saying that he never had sex in that fashion before. I told him to look at it as another acting gig. It was the constant nude pictures you took of me being tied to the bed with my pussy on full display and with me tied down on all fours that made him change his mind. He believed me after you sent him those pics. By doing that, he had no choice but to give in to the perverse sexual act. I'm still debating if I should send them to an S&M magazine or not. I could get paid for 'em. They were that good." Kharma laughed.

I was too tuned in to what was on the phone to laugh with her. Evan should've left me alone on the account of I had him at my mercy now, and he didn't even know it. If he had not tried to mess me over with my former P.O., then I wouldn't be on the shit I was on. He started it and now I was about to finish it. Kharma passed me some earbuds to plug into the phone so I could hear the audio. I watched and listened intently. Without a doubt, the average eye and ear would think this was none other than a rape occurring. I gave Kharma her credit, she sold that shit. For her acting abilities, I should introduce her to Lil' B. If she had asked for more money, I would've kindly have given it to her. She deserved it. I paid her the remaining money I owed her, and we departed to never see each other again. Now it was time for part three.

I anonymously shared the video with the police, TMZ, Dish Nation, CNN, The Real, all local news stations in Atlanta, and anybody else who would publicly show the video and talk about it. Yes! Yes! Yes! Vengeance is mine!

******

It took all of three days for Evan's sex tape, or shall we call it, rape tape to hit full circulation. It was the cover story on every news outlet in the country. CBS, ABC, NBC, CNN, and any other major news station I could think of at the moment covered the story. Even Trump and his latest bullshit hadn't covered more than the bullshit Evan was in. Every newspaper in the country had a different headline for Evan and his apparent rape. Evan was the most talked about subject on social media. Everybody was casting their judgements and opinions of him. As of now, there were no charges brought against him, however, Atlanta Police were conducting a full investigation.

I was sitting in my living room alone watching the news one day when a breaking news announcement came across the screen. It pertained to Evan. I crossed my fingers, hoping they'd finally charged him. What they were talking about was even better. Two more women had come forward with allegations that they'd been raped by Evan. Oh, it was about to be a for sure domino effect now. Watch what I tell you. There always is in high profile cases like these. I was sitting there smiling from ear to ear, when all of sudden, I burst into laughter, screaming at my television.

"Now take that, bitch! Who gets the last laugh? Me, that's who!" I laughed for a good minute or two.

In the coming weeks, ten more women came forward with claims that Evan either sexually assaulted them, or he committed sexual misconduct in some form or fashion. Four of the women chose to remain anonymous while the other six said that they were no longer afraid of Evan. All they wanted was justice. One of the women was a well-known actress and was assaulted by Evan one night she'd been at his hotel room going over a script with him.

Evan and his high-profile attorneys denied all allegations against him, citing that their client was being targeted by some money-seeking women, claiming that Evan was the real victim. They vowed to fight to the end to clear Evan's name. Tia was devastated by it all. Evan had to cut her off. He had to. He could no longer support her with the condo, so she had to move out of it. He let her keep the car since it was already paid for. I felt kinda bad for her. Be that as it may, it was good she knew the real person she'd been dealing with. I let her move in with me for however long she needed to. I didn't care how long it would take her to get her own place, she was always welcomed at mine. She walked around the apartment sulking day in and day out. I had to force her to get out of the apartment so she could have some fun and possibly meet somebody new. I know some of you are like, "Bitch, please! Gone somewhere with all that. You the very reason she lost everything in the first place, so it's only right that she lives with you." I can feel that. But I know there are some of you who can understand why I did what I did. It was all good. At whatever cost, I got my revenge. Sometimes, innocent people have to get caught in the crossfire. It was just life.

Chapter Twenty-Two
Three Months Later...

Kahari and I were now living together. We had been for almost a month and a half now. We had the perfect relationship. I did everything I could, to please my man, to make him smile, to take away the stress that constantly crept into his life. I'm not going to front. Some nights I loved when he came home all worked up about something pertaining to his street business and he takes that shit out on me. He won't strike up an argument or put his hands on me or nothing like that. What he does is beat the hell out of my pussy. He would take me aggressively, and domineering, and it would have my pussy flooding every time he did. Real talk, sometimes, I would secretly pray that somebody would come up short with his money or this or that business deal didn't fall through for him, or that somebody played him to the left. I knew if that happened, then he would punish my pussy in a good way. I was great for Kahari and he was even greater for me. We lifted each other up whenever one lacked the energy or confidence to lift ourselves up. He had my back in whatever, as long as that whatever didn't have a potential trip to prison written all over it. Kahari has indeed taught me how to love, how to surrender my heart to him like the song goes. I cooked for him. Let me be real, I tried to cook for him because I couldn't cook to save my life, but it was the thought that counted, right? I had his bath water warm for him just the way he liked. I massage him, give him head whenever he asked, and I do mean whenever. We could be driving down the interstate, any street, or wherever. If he wanted it, I was diving headfirst like a scuba diver. There was nothing I wouldn't do for him. If he ever asked me to kill someone for him, their ass is as good as dead. All that I had done for him and would do for him was on a mutual level of respect.

He cooked for me. Yes, he threw down in the kitchen. It was one of his many talents. He bathed me. He rubbed my body from top to bottom. No one had ever massaged my head while making love to me at the same time. I loved it when he did that. It was by far the most incredible feeling I've ever felt. Kahari has a way of making me feel like I had never felt before. He did everything he could, to make me happy and appreciated. He loved me just as much as I loved him. We lived in a four-bedroom house in the Dellwood area. It was a nice community, calm and reserved, not a lot of violence taking place. I loved it. I left my apartment to Tia. It was the least I could do considering the circumstances. I still had a key however, but I respected her privacy enough to when I went over there, I knocked first. She was still trying to find her identity after the whole Evan ordeal. It literally turned her life upside down. Especially after prosecutors in L.A., New York, and Miami were charging him with rape and sexual misconduct. There were a total of thirty women who'd come forward on Evan. Tia still hasn't heard a word from him, but she held onto hope that one day she would. In spite of her still hurting, I knew that it would be a matter of time before she bounced back. She was a hustler and she taught me how to make it in this cruel world. I hold her in high regard, so I wasn't tripping on me still paying the rent. Kahari even chipped in to help her, which I thought was sweet of him to help my best friend in her time of need. She was here tonight at me and Kahari's place along with Black, Rachel, Shamarah, and two girls from the Blue Flame, celebrating with me.

Tonight, the premiere of season five of *Love N Da Hood* was airing on VH1. I had been told by Pamela and a few producers that I'd done a fantastic job. We were already in talks about me coming back for season six. Pamela predicted that America was going to love me unconditionally once the season aired. I sure hoped so because I still had to get my role in Lil' B's movie. Speaking of him, we stayed in touch over the months. The last time I talked to him was last week. He said, hopefully he would start shooting my scenes soon. He was just waiting on confirmation from the viewers. I had the role wrapped around my pinkie if that was the case. Lil' B also told me that he had to get someone else to play the role Evan was playing and re-shoot the scenes. Turns out, a lot of important people had to distance themselves from Evan.

Anyway, we watched *Love N Da Hood*. They did a live feed for the fans to cast their thoughts and opinions. I was getting so much positive feedback every time I was shown. Most people wanted to know who I was, some were saying how fine I was for a white girl, wondering if my butt was real or not. Some wanted me to get beat up by Yasmin and Alisa. They had to be fans of them, but I still got the attention I wanted. It was all love. I loved seeing myself on TV. The camera does make you look ten pounds thicker. I didn't look fat. I was super fine for my first time on TV. I even heard Black telling Kahari, "Bruh, you got some fine swine in Nikki."

I laughed when I heard him say that. He was always calling me swine. Hell, he called all white women swine. One day I asked him his reason for calling us that, and he didn't hesitate with his answer. "You know how swine is good to the black man when he's eatin' it, but after he's done eatin' it, it's not good for the black man in the long run 'cause it causes all kinds of health problems an' shit?"

"So, you sayin' I'm not good for Kahari? Is that what you're sayin'?" I asked. Again, Black was quick with his answer.

"Let's not make what I say about you and Kahari. Datz my boy. If he's happy then datz all dat matters. Me callin' white women swine is a term dat I use, not him. So, try not to make a big deal about it."

I wasn't trying to make a big deal out of it, so I just laughed it off, telling him I felt him. I just wanted to know why. It really humored me to be honest. Bet you he doesn't call Rachel that shit when he's dicking her down. I asked her myself and she said he didn't. Rachel was cheating on her boyfriend with Black every chance she got. She liked Black a lot, but she wasn't going to break up with her boyfriend for him. Her boyfriend was a welder and made a pretty decent living from it working for this big-time welding company. She knew Black was good to her in the bedroom, but he wasn't good for her. When *Love N Da Hood* went off, we talked about me, Rachel, and Shamarah being on TV and what everyone thought about us. Not long after, everybody started to leave. I told my girls I would talk to them later. I thought Kahari and I were about to enjoy some alone time, but he said he had to make a run and wouldn't be back for at least an hour or two. It was already kinda late to begin with. I whispered in his ear to be safe and when he returned, I was going to suck his dick until he broke a toe or two. Then I was going to let him fuck me anyway he chose for the remainder of the night.

"Bet dat up," he said, kissing me and palming my big juicy booty. "I'll be back."

He walked out of our house. I cleaned up the plates of food we ate, washed the dishes, then jumped in the shower. Afterwards, I went on Instagram to see if my followers had watched tonight's episode. They all had, and they'd left positive feedback about how I did. They showed me so much love, made me tear up a bit. I went live and they continued to pour out their blessings to me. I even seen Lil' B on my feed, posting the muscle arm and 100 emojis. Then, he wrote, job well done! I went to his DM, thanking him. He messaged back saying that I'd done great and the role was mine.

"To be honest, the role has always been yours from the moment I saw you."

I screamed in happiness, jumping up and down on the bed like a little kid. I sent Lil' B back at least ten emojis of kissing lips and hearts then returned to my live-feed to tell everyone the good news about my future acting career and to be on the lookout for me because I was coming. I stayed on for about forty-five minutes before shutting down for the night. I was getting sleepy and was about to turn it in. I couldn't wait for Kahari to come home so I could tell him that his boo was about to be a movie star. Except my world then flipped upside down.

I woke up close to 3 a.m. because I smelled Tia all over me. I know that perfume from anywhere. I thought she was in my bed and turned over to see why, only to see Kahari lying there fast asleep. Why did he smell like her? It should have been obvious why he smelled like her, but everyone deserves a chance to explain themselves, right? Maybe he had a good explanation why he had her perfume all over him. I hope the two of them weren't playing me to the left in any kind of way. Particularly, Tia. She better not be there, has already taken it there, or was thinking about taking it there with me. She better not be anywhere close to there. I would never forgive her if she had been stabbing me in my back this whole time. I woke Kahari up asking him why the hell he had Tia's smell on him.

He calmly stated that she'd called him while he was out handling his business and she called and asked would he come help her move a bed out of the guestroom for her, so he and Black stopped by to help her. He said he was too tired to take a shower when he got back in. I peered at him, searching for any sign of fuckery. I couldn't find one. I had no choice but to believe him.

"Now, can I go back to bed, Inspector gadget?" he asked playfully, causing me to smile.

"I'm just sayin'. Come in here with a woman's perfume all over you. I thought I was finna have to fuck both of y'all up." I was more than serious.

"Well, you don't have to do none of that Jackie Chan. Now go back to sleep."

"Not until you wash her smell off of you."

"Are you serious?!"

I folded my arms, showing him that I was. He mumbled something but got out of bed to go take a shower. While he was in it, I moved quickly, searching through his pants and phone. I checked the call log. There was a call from Tia at 1:22 a.m. I went through his texts. Nothing. I was a bit sketchy of Kahari. He was smart and cautiously meticulous in the way that he moved. He wouldn't slip and have her perfume on him like that if they'd been doing anything. Maybe I was overreacting. I eased up on my paranoia and relaxed, getting back into bed. When Kahari came back in drying himself, he asked me if I had found what I was looking for.

"Found what I was lookin' for? I don't know what you mean by that," I knew what he was referring to.

"In my phone. I know you been in there, Jew. You find your evidence?"

"Boy, I haven't touched your phone."

"Yea, whatever. I'm about to go to sleep," he said, climbing into bed, dick swinging back and forth. As soon as he got under the covers, I reached for it.

"Don't even try it. Access denied," he said, pushing my hand away.

"Ungh, Baeee!"

"Bae, hell. Go to sleep Karolina. Yo' ass on dick restriction for the next three days." He turned over on his side, facing away from me.

"Bae, nooo! Don't do me like that."

"You done it to yourself, Jew. Goodnight." With that, he had no more words for me. Guess what I did? I played with my pussy while he laid there acting like he didn't hear me. I made sure I was very vocal and loud.

"Mmmm shit! Feels so good. Pussy so wet. Ooouu, Baeee, I wish you could be inside of me, fuckin' me with that big dick of yours. Oooouuu-fuck! Ahh-ahhh-ahhhh!" I threw my leg on him and fingered myself faster. "Oh, good God, it feels so good. Turn over baby and fuck me. Punish me for comin' at you the way that I did. Please! Oooohhh. My. Godddd!" I pulled my fingers out and began sucking on them. ". Mmmmm I taste delicious. You want some baby?"

Next thing I know, I heard Kahari snore. No, he didn't. Motherfucker! Oh well, no need in letting a good orgasm go to waste. I continued fingering myself until I came all over my fingers. I licked my fingers dry then turned over and went to sleep, holding my man.

I woke up early the next morning, and to my surprise, thoughts of Kahari and Tia were on my mind. I tried to let the thought of them getting it on together behind my back go. No matter how hard I tried, it just wouldn't leave. Kahari was still asleep. I looked at the time on my phone. Tia should be up by now. I texted her good morning with the coffee cup emoji. She texted me right back with the same emoji. I asked her what she had planned for today because I'd just got off the phone with Lil' B and he wanted me to fly to L.A. tomorrow. I lied like he wanted me to meet someone very important. She called me after that.

"So, you're really becomin' a star in the making, aren't you?"

"That's what it looks like. I can't begin to explain how I feel."

"You were awesome last night."

"Speakin' of last night, Kahari said you called him to come over to help you move your refrigerator 'cause you thought you had seen a snake go under it."

"Yea, I did. I was scared out of my mind. You know how I feel about snakes," she said.

My heart dropped, shattering into a million pieces. This couldn't be true. My best friend who I loved like a sister played Judas on me. I wanted to cry as I stared into space. "Get it together, Nikki," I said to myself at least twenty times. Although the truth was made known that she and Kahari were definitely fucking last night, I still wanted more proof. Come to think about it, there was no telling how long they've been sleeping together. I wanted to catch them in the act like we were on an episode of Cheaters. I needed to develop a plan to catch them. I heard my line beep and when I looked at the screen, it was Lil' B. I told Tia I had to take his call, hanging up on her without so much of a goodbye or I'll talk to you later. I gathered all the strength I had before answering.

"Good mornin', Mister. What's got you callin' me this time of the mornin'?" I was trying to muster up a cheerful tone.

"I need you to come to Columbus today."

"Columbus, Georgia?" I was curious. He was talking about his hometown Columbus, Mississippi. It was a four-hour drive from Atlanta. "May I ask why?"

"I got some important people I need you to meet."

Well I be damned, I thought. He was just lying to Tia not even five minutes ago about Lil' B wanting me to fly to L.A., and here he was actually wanting me to come to Mississippi. Was the Lord trying to tell me something? It sure felt like He was. It was a coincidence, but a much-needed distraction, nonetheless. I asked him how long he wanted me to stay.

"Two, three days, max."

"As soon as I pack, I'll be on my way," I promised and hung up.

I went to wake up Kahari's two-timing, cheating ass to tell him I had to go to Mississippi. I'd been close to going to the kitchen, grabbing a knife, and stabbing him a hundred ways to hell. Weak motherfucker! I thought about it and started packing my things. He offered to come with me, but I could tell it was in a halfhearted effort. He didn't want to come. No, he wanted to be with Tia. Ugh! I had to stop packing and get myself together. I almost lost it. He asked me if I was alright.

"I'm fine. Just tired is all."

I couldn't wait to get away from him. I got everything I needed and left. I had to give him a fake kiss and all.

"Are you sure you're alright, baby?"

Just yesterday, hearing him call me baby made my heart flutter and made my pussy super wet. Hearing him now, made me cringe. To be real, I had murderous thoughts. I hurried up and left. I stopped by Rachel's first to tell her everything. She wanted to go jump on Tia right then and there. I told her not yet, to give it time. She said in the meantime while I was out of town, she would ride by my old apartment occasionally to see if Kahari's car was parked outside. If it was, she was going to give me a call. I thought that was a great idea.

"I got you, Cuz. You just be careful on that highway, alright?"

"I will," I promised then left her place to go fill up my tank.

Zion

Chapter Twenty-Three

Just after I arrived in Columbus, Mississippi, I met with Lil' B in a suite at the Wingate Hotel. Lil' B had it for me to stay there while I was in town. I asked him where the people where he wanted me to meet. He told me they weren't due in until tomorrow.

"Kick back and relax some. Get some rest if you need to. Enjoy a massage and the spa. Do whatever to clear your mind," he said.

"What do you mean by your last comment? My mind is clear," I said, knowing that it wasn't.

Lil' B looked at me as if he didn't believe me. "Come sit down with me," He offered, leading me to the sofa. "I'm good with vibes, feeling peoples' energy, knowin' how to read their body language. You've had a frown on your face since you've arrived. Usually, you're all smiles and uppity in your demeanor. Lookin' at you now, it looks like you're about to kill somebody. It isn't me, is it? Do I need to be afraid of you right now?" He asked in a fun-loving way.

"No, silly. You know I wouldn't bring any harm to you. It's just that I found out something about my boyfriend and best friend. I think they're fuckin' around behind my back and it's eatin' me up inside."

"Do you think, or do you know?"

"What if I say both? Is that even possible?" I breathed out heavily, sighing my stupidity. I had been the biggest fool on earth. Two people who I would lay down my life for were treating me like an ass. A birdbrain. A bonehead. A lamebrain. God, I was an idiot. I became mad all over again. I was angrier than before. I slammed my fist on the coffee table then burst into a sob. Lil' B wrapped his arms around me, rubbing my back as he told me to stop crying because everything was going to be alright.

"No, it's not. This is the first time I've ever loved a man the way that I love Kahari. Love is not supposed to feel like this," I wailed, tears wetting Lil' B's Polo shirt. He didn't seem to mind. He was genuinely concerned with my feelings, helping to downplay the situation.

"As bad as it sounds, love is supposed to hurt. It's a number of things, really. My wife taught me how to be patient with love. How to sacrifice for it. The way I started out lovin' her was the most hurt she's ever suffered. Don't get me wrong, she hurt me too, and I've never known hurt like that. But we rode it out and stuck with each other through it all. You know what really got my wife and I here more than love?"

"Wh-what?"

"Forgiveness. When you love someone, there's goin' to come a time when you have to forgive that person. That person will have to forgive you as well. There's no way around it. Now sit up straight so I can see you."

I wanted to remain in his embrace. I felt safe there. However, I sat up straight like he asked.

"Nikki, you're loved. You're beautiful. And you're gifted. You have a lot of life left in you, so I suggest you live it. You're goin' to have the opportunity to love the perfect man, and he's goin' to be more than willing to love you back."

It was amazing how Lil' B always saw the good in me.

"Hold out your hands for me, will ya?" he said.

I held them out for him wondering why he wanted me to. "In your left hand is your personal life. Family, friends, and loved ones. In your right hand, you're holding your business life. Your job, your career, your future, and all the opportunities you have before you. Both of them are important to you, but one actually outweighs the other. Which one is it?

186

You don't have to answer the question to me. One of these days you're goin' to have to answer it to yourself."

I was staring at my hands, waiting to see which one would drop first. I felt the weight shift in my right hand and what do I do? I let both hands fall, not wanting to disappoint Lil' B. I didn't want him to think that I wasn't about my business. I thanked him for his wisdom, explaining to him that I understood where he was coming from. We stood up and hugged before he walked out, leaving me to my personal problems. I went to take a shower. Under the warm water, I cried like a baby. Why did my best friend and boyfriend have to hurt me like this?

******

"His car is parked right beside hers."

"Are you sure it's his?" I asked Rachel. She was being my spy like she promised she would be.

"Of course, I'm sure. I'm lookin' right at it. I know Kahari's car when I see it," she confirmed.

Tears welled in my eyes. The anger burned my insides. "Any idea how long he's been there?"

"Nope. What do you want me to do? I tell you what. I'm fixin' to go knock on the door and act like I was in the neighborhood and decided to stop by."

I could leave it up to Rachel to come up with the best ideas. She told me she would call me back and hung up. Meanwhile, I paced the floor, walking in circles, and biting my nails. I threw punches in the air, imagining Tia's face I was connecting with. I knew I should've killed Kahari this morning when I had the chance, instead of giving him the chance to cheat on me some more. He'd called me about an hour ago asking what I was doing then got off the phone with

187

me. I fell to the floor on my ass, crying like a baby all over again. I had to stop with all this gotdamn crying. It was killing me. It wasn't like my tears would make reality go away. Still, I cried. Rachel called me back exactly twelve minutes and twenty-three seconds later, saying that she could hear them from the outside of the apartment having sex. She said she was able to get Tia to answer the door and let her in because she told her she really had to use the bathroom. Rachel said she could smell sex all in the apartment. When she asked Tia who she was getting it in with, Tia told her that Evan had snuck in town to see her.

"She rushed me out of there fast. Cuz, I'm sorry, but they're in there fuckin' as we speak. It took everything in me not to confront them."

That was it. I couldn't take it anymore. I hung up the phone, grabbing my suitcases and bolted out of the suite like a bat out of hell. I was heading back to Atlanta. It was a little after 4 a.m. when I parked my car three cars down from Tia's and Kahari's. It was definitely Kahari's car. I walked fast to the upstairs apartment. Quietly as possible, I put the key in the lock and turned the knob. What the hell?! These motherfuckers were still going at it. I could hear Tia loud and clear.

"Take it out and put it in my ass, Kahari! That's it! Mmmmhhh!" The million pieces that my heart broke into from yesterday's discovery, those pieces were now breaking into millions of their own. I gasped for breath. Felt like I was having a panic attack, a heart attack even. I had to sit down. All the while, I tried blocking out Tia's cries of passion.

"Ahhhh! Ye-yeah! All of it! I want to feel every inch inside of me. Put all that dick in my tight ass, boyyyy!"

"Like, dis?"

"Ooouuu, yessss, like that! Just like that, Kahari! Don't stop! Fuck my ass harder!"

That's it. I couldn't stand to hear another sound coming from them. If I knew Kahari correctly, he had a gun hidden under the cushions of the couch. He always kept one there in our home for security purposes no matter what. I checked and just like I figured, one was there. I was terrified of guns but not now. No sir. No ma'am. I'd held this same gun in my hand before when Kahari was trying to teach me how to hold it and use it. I remember asking him why he wanted to teach me such a thing.

"You never know when you'll have to use it. It's for your own protection."

So, I cocked back the hammer, securing a bullet in the chamber the way he'd taught me. Tia's bedroom, my old bedroom, door was open. I could see Kahari pounding her hard from the back as she cried out for him to keep fucking her ass hard like he was. I aimed the gun.

"This how y'all do me, huh?"

They both jumped in surprise, Kahari trying to reach for his gun. He didn't know who I was. I shot him in the back twice before he could get to it, watching him slump over. Tia burst into a cry, begging me not to shoot her as I walked closer to the bed.

"Please, Nikki! Don't kill me! I'm sorry!"

I wasn't about to have one of those long, drawn out talks with her like they do in the movies before killing someone. I didn't hesitate to shoot her four times in the face. I could hear Kahari struggling for breath, clinging on to his pathetic life. I put the barrel of the gun to the back of his head and blew his fucking brains out. I backed up, panting hard. I'd killed my best friend and boyfriend, two people who meant the world to me. I started crying again. Shortly after, I heard sirens in the background. I knew they were coming for me. I wasn't going back to prison. I meant every word when I said I was never going back under any circumstances. I raised the gun to my head and pulled the trigger. Miraculously, nothing happened. The gun had jammed. I tried pulling the trigger again and again. Still, nothing. I fell to my knees crying until the police came in to arrest me. The rest of that morning went by in a blur.

When I came to, I sat in the Fulton County jail. I was charged with double homicide and was given no bond. Detectives came to talk to me, but I had no words for them. I had no words for no one. My life was over. I let everybody down. Me, my family, friends, and Lil' B. Everybody who cared about me and loved me, I broke their hearts. I'm sorry you guys, forgive me. I did what I thought was best, but all I'd done was throw my life away. My career. All of it. Love is no joke and I found that out the hard way. Too bad I would never get to love again. Maybe that was a good thing.

I was sentenced to life in prison without the possibility of parole. I leave these words with all you young women out there, that's a model or stripper, don't let your life become mine. I regret my whole life. I didn't even bother to try and reach out to Ro. I knew I couldn't count on him to hold me down. Men aren't built like that. Guess I'll talk to you guys later. I gotta go start on this time. How I'ma do it? One day at a time.

The End.

Submission Guideline

Submit the first three chapters of your completed manuscript to ldpsubmissions@gmail.com, subject line: Your book's title. The manuscript must be in a .doc file and sent as an attachment. Document should be in Times New Roman, double spaced and in size 12 font. Also, provide your synopsis and full contact information. If sending multiple submissions, they must each be in a separate email.

Have a story but no way to send it electronically? You can still submit to LDP/Ca$h Presents. Send in the first three chapters, written or typed, of your completed manuscript to:

LDP: Submissions Dept
Po Box 944
Stockbridge, Ga 30281

DO NOT send original manuscript. Must be a duplicate.

Provide your synopsis and a cover letter containing your full contact information.

Thanks for considering LDP and Ca$h Presents.

Coming Soon from Lock Down Publications/Ca$h Presents

BOW DOWN TO MY GANGSTA

By **Ca$h**

TORN BETWEEN TWO

By **Coffee**

THE STREETS STAINED MY SOUL **II**

By **Marcellus Allen**

BLOOD OF A BOSS **VI**

SHADOWS OF THE GAME II

By **Askari**

LOYAL TO THE GAME **IV**

By **T.J. & Jelissa**

A DOPEBOY'S PRAYER **II**

By **Eddie "Wolf" Lee**

IF LOVING YOU IS WRONG… **III**

By **Jelissa**

TRUE SAVAGE **VII**

MIDNIGHT CARTEL III

DOPE BOY MAGIC IV

CITY OF KINGZ II

By **Chris Green**

BLAST FOR ME **III**

A SAVAGE DOPEBOY III

CUTTHROAT MAFIA III

By **Ghost**

A HUSTLER'S DECEIT III

KILL ZONE **II**

BAE BELONGS TO ME III

A DOPE BOY'S QUEEN III

By **Aryanna**

COKE KINGS V

KING OF THE TRAP II

By **T.J. Edwards**

GORILLAZ IN THE BAY V

De'Kari

THE STREETS ARE CALLING II

Duquie Wilson

KINGPIN KILLAZ IV

STREET KINGS III

PAID IN BLOOD III

CARTEL KILLAZ IV

DOPE GODS III

Hood Rich

SINS OF A HUSTLA II

ASAD

KINGZ OF THE GAME V

Playa Ray

SLAUGHTER GANG IV

RUTHLESS HEART IV

By Willie Slaughter

THE HEART OF A SAVAGE III

By Jibril Williams

FUK SHYT II

By Blakk Diamond
THE REALEST KILLAZ III
By Tranay Adams
TRAP GOD III
By Troublesome
YAYO IV
A SHOOTER'S AMBITION III
By S. Allen
GHOST MOB
Stilloan Robinson
KINGPIN DREAMS III
By Paper Boi Rari
CREAM II
By Yolanda Moore
SON OF A DOPE FIEND III
By Renta
FOREVER GANGSTA II
GLOCKS ON SATIN SHEETS III
By Adrian Dulan
LOYALTY AIN'T PROMISED II
By Keith Williams
THE PRICE YOU PAY FOR LOVE II
By Destiny Skai
CONFESSIONS OF A GANGSTA II
By Nicholas Lock
I'M NOTHING WITHOUT HIS LOVE II
SINS OF A THUG II

By Monet Dragun

LIFE OF A SAVAGE IV

A GANGSTA'S QUR'AN III

MURDA SEASON III

GANGLAND CARTEL II

By **Romell Tukes**

QUIET MONEY III

THUG LIFE II

By **Trai'Quan**

THE STREETS MADE ME III

By **Larry D. Wright**

THE ULTIMATE SACRIFICE VI

IF YOU CROSS ME ONCE II

ANGEL III

By **Anthony Fields**

THE LIFE OF A HOOD STAR

By Ca$h & Rashia Wilson

FRIEND OR FOE II

By **Mimi**

SAVAGE STORMS II

By **Meesha**

BLOOD ON THE MONEY II

By J-Blunt

THE STREETS WILL NEVER CLOSE II

By **K'ajji**

NIGHTMARES OF A HUSTLA II

By King Dream

Available Now

RESTRAINING ORDER **I & II**
By **CA$H & Coffee**
LOVE KNOWS NO BOUNDARIES **I II & III**
By **Coffee**
RAISED AS A GOON I, II, III & IV
BRED BY THE SLUMS I, II, III
BLAST FOR ME I & II
ROTTEN TO THE CORE I II III
A BRONX TALE I, II, III
DUFFEL BAG CARTEL I II III IV
HEARTLESS GOON I II III IV
A SAVAGE DOPEBOY I II
HEARTLESS GOON I II III
DRUG LORDS I II III
CUTTHROAT MAFIA I II
By **Ghost**
LAY IT DOWN **I & II**
LAST OF A DYING BREED
BLOOD STAINS OF A SHOTTA I & II III
By **Jamaica**
LOYAL TO THE GAME I II III
LIFE OF SIN I, II III
By **TJ & Jelissa**
BLOODY COMMAS I & II
SKI MASK CARTEL I II & III

KING OF NEW YORK I II,III IV V

RISE TO POWER I II III

COKE KINGS I II III IV

BORN HEARTLESS I II III IV

KING OF THE TRAP

By **T.J. Edwards**

IF LOVING HIM IS WRONG…I & II

LOVE ME EVEN WHEN IT HURTS I II III

By **Jelissa**

WHEN THE STREETS CLAP BACK I & II III

THE HEART OF A SAVAGE I II

By **Jibril Williams**

A DISTINGUISHED THUG STOLE MY HEART I II & III

LOVE SHOULDN'T HURT I II III IV

RENEGADE BOYS I II III IV

PAID IN KARMA I II III

SAVAGE STORMS

By **Meesha**

A GANGSTER'S CODE I &, II III

A GANGSTER'S SYN I II III

THE SAVAGE LIFE I II III

CHAINED TO THE STREETS I II III

BLOOD ON THE MONEY

By **J-Blunt**

PUSH IT TO THE LIMIT

By **Bre' Hayes**

BLOOD OF A BOSS **I, II, III, IV, V**

SHADOWS OF THE GAME

By **Askari**

THE STREETS BLEED MURDER **I, II & III**

THE HEART OF A GANGSTA I II& III

By **Jerry Jackson**

CUM FOR ME I II III IV V VI

An **LDP Erotica Collaboration**

BRIDE OF A HUSTLA **I II & II**

THE FETTI GIRLS **I, II& III**

CORRUPTED BY A GANGSTA I, II III, IV

BLINDED BY HIS LOVE

THE PRICE YOU PAY FOR LOVE

DOPE GIRL MAGIC I II III

By **Destiny Skai**

WHEN A GOOD GIRL GOES BAD

By **Adrienne**

THE COST OF LOYALTY I II III

By Kweli

A GANGSTER'S REVENGE **I II III & IV**

THE BOSS MAN'S DAUGHTERS I II III IV V

A SAVAGE LOVE **I & II**

BAE BELONGS TO ME I II

A HUSTLER'S DECEIT I, II, III

WHAT BAD BITCHES DO I, II, III

SOUL OF A MONSTER I II III

KILL ZONE

A DOPE BOY'S QUEEN I II

By **Aryanna**

A KINGPIN'S AMBITON

A KINGPIN'S AMBITION **II**

I MURDER FOR THE DOUGH

By **Ambitious**

TRUE SAVAGE I II III IV V VI

DOPE BOY MAGIC I, II, III

MIDNIGHT CARTEL I II

CITY OF KINGZ

By **Chris Green**

A DOPEBOY'S PRAYER

By **Eddie "Wolf" Lee**

THE KING CARTEL **I, II & III**

By **Frank Gresham**

THESE NIGGAS AIN'T LOYAL **I, II & III**

By **Nikki Tee**

GANGSTA SHYT **I II &III**

By **CATO**

THE ULTIMATE BETRAYAL

By **Phoenix**

BOSS'N UP **I , II & III**

By **Royal Nicole**

I LOVE YOU TO DEATH

By Destiny J

I RIDE FOR MY HITTA

I STILL RIDE FOR MY HITTA

By **Misty Holt**

LOVE & CHASIN' PAPER

By **Qay Crockett**

TO DIE IN VAIN

SINS OF A HUSTLA

By **ASAD**

BROOKLYN HUSTLAZ

By **Boogsy Morina**

BROOKLYN ON LOCK I & II

By **Sonovia**

GANGSTA CITY

By **Teddy Duke**

A DRUG KING AND HIS DIAMOND I & II III

A DOPEMAN'S RICHES

HER MAN, MINE'S TOO I, II

CASH MONEY HO'S

By Nicole Goosby

TRAPHOUSE KING **I II & III**

KINGPIN KILLAZ I II III

STREET KINGS I II

PAID IN BLOOD **I II**

CARTEL KILLAZ I II III

DOPE GODS I II

By **Hood Rich**

LIPSTICK KILLAH **I, II, III**

CRIME OF PASSION I II & III

FRIEND OR FOE

By **Mimi**

200

STEADY MOBBN' **I, II, III**

THE STREETS STAINED MY SOUL

By **Marcellus Allen**

WHO SHOT YA **I, II, III**

SON OF A DOPE FIEND I II

Renta

GORILLAZ IN THE BAY **I II III IV**

TEARS OF A GANGSTA I II

DE'KARI

TRIGGADALE I II III

Elijah R. Freeman

GOD BLESS THE TRAPPERS I, II, III

THESE SCANDALOUS STREETS I, II, III

FEAR MY GANGSTA I, II, III IV, V

THESE STREETS DON'T LOVE NOBODY I, II

BURY ME A G I, II, III, IV, V

A GANGSTA'S EMPIRE I, II, III, IV

THE DOPEMAN'S BODYGAURD I II

THE REALEST KILLAZ I II

Tranay Adams

THE STREETS ARE CALLING

Duquie Wilson

MARRIED TO A BOSS… I II III

By Destiny Skai & Chris Green

KINGZ OF THE GAME I II III IV

Playa Ray

SLAUGHTER GANG I II III

RUTHLESS HEART I II III

By Willie Slaughter

FUK SHYT

By Blakk Diamond

DON'T F#CK WITH MY HEART I II

By Linnea

ADDICTED TO THE DRAMA I II III

By Jamila

YAYO I II III

A SHOOTER'S AMBITION I II

By S. Allen

TRAP GOD I II

By Troublesome

FOREVER GANGSTA

GLOCKS ON SATIN SHEETS I II

By Adrian Dulan

TOE TAGZ I II III

By Ah'Million

KINGPIN DREAMS I II

By Paper Boi Rari

CONFESSIONS OF A GANGSTA

By Nicholas Lock

I'M NOTHING WITHOUT HIS LOVE

SINS OF A THUG

By Monet Dragun

CAUGHT UP IN THE LIFE I II III

By Robert Baptiste

NEW TO THE GAME I II III
By **Malik D. Rice**
LIFE OF A SAVAGE I II III
A GANGSTA'S QUR'AN I II
MURDA SEASON I II
GANGLAND CARTEL
By **Romell Tukes**
LOYALTY AIN'T PROMISED
By Keith Williams
QUIET MONEY I II
THUG LIFE
By **Trai'Quan**
THE STREETS MADE ME I II
By **Larry D. Wright**
THE ULTIMATE SACRIFICE I, II, III, IV, V
KHADIFI
IF YOU CROSS ME ONCE
ANGEL I II
By **Anthony Fields**
THE LIFE OF A HOOD STAR
By Ca$h & Rashia Wilson
THE STREETS WILL NEVER CLOSE
By K'ajji
CREAM
By Yolanda Moore
NIGHTMARES OF A HUSTLA
By King Dream

<u>BOOKS BY LDP'S CEO, CA$H</u>

<u>TRUST IN NO MAN</u>

<u>TRUST IN NO MAN 2</u>

<u>TRUST IN NO MAN 3</u>

<u>BONDED BY BLOOD</u>

<u>SHORTY GOT A THUG</u>

<u>THUGS CRY</u>

<u>THUGS CRY 2</u>

<u>THUGS CRY 3</u>

<u>TRUST NO BITCH</u>

<u>TRUST NO BITCH 2</u>

<u>TRUST NO BITCH 3</u>

<u>TIL MY CASKET DROPS</u>

<u>RESTRAINING ORDER</u>

<u>RESTRAINING ORDER 2</u>

<u>IN LOVE WITH A CONVICT</u>

<u>LIFE OF A HOOD STAR</u>

<u>Coming Soon</u>

BONDED BY BLOOD 2

BOW DOWN TO MY GANGSTA

9 781952 936555